# aperture

The Magazine of Photography and Ideas

FULFILLMENT CENTER
711 SPENCE LANE
NASHVILLE, TN 37217

PERIODICAL
U.S. POSTAGE PAID
NEW YORK, NY
AND ADDITIONAL
MAILING OFFICES

POSTAL APPROVED POLY

#256

#BXNHYKF ************************5-DIGIT 10010
#02031078# SPR26 #262 P7 APE
SEVERN TAYLOR
205 E 22ND ST APT 5F
NEW YORK, NY 10010-4622

P-1  P24-151

**DO NOT BEND**

MAROMA
A BELMOND HOTEL
RIVIERA MAYA

Robert Adams

Diane Arbus

Bernd & Hilla Becher

Elisheva Biernoff

Mel Bochner

Sophie Calle

Cardiff & Miller

Liz Deschenes

Kota Ezawa

Lee Friedlander

Adam Fuss

Nan Goldin

Katy Grannan

Martine Gutierrez

Peter Hujar

Richard Learoyd

Helen Levitt

Christian Marclay

Wardell Milan

Richard Misrach

Nicholas Nixon

Alec Soth

Hiroshi Sugimoto

Richard T. Walker

Carrie Mae Weems

Garry Winogrand

fraenkelgallery.com

FRÆNKEL

DIANE ARBUS, *Teenager with a baseball bat, N.Y.C. 1962*

# Arrhythmic Mythic Ra
# Fall 2024

## Columns

28

## Features

77

90

Front cover:
Lieko Shiga, *Untitled*, 2024

# Features

74

# The PhotoBook Review

138

Subscribe to *Aperture* and
read more at aperture.org.

# aperture

The Magazine of Photography and Ideas

Editor in Chief
**Michael Famighetti**
Associate Managing Editor
**Zack Hatfield**
Contributing Editor
**Brendan Embser**
Contributing Editor, The PhotoBook Review
**Noa Lin**
Copy Editors
**Hilary Becker, Donna Ghelerter, Chris Peterson**
Production Director
**Minjee Cho**
Production Manager
**Andrea Chlad**
Press Supervisor
**Ali Taptık**

Art Direction, Design & Typefaces
**A2/SW/HK, London**

Publisher
**Dana Triwush**
magazine@aperture.org

Director of Corporate Partnerships
**Flynn Murray**
fmurray@aperture.org

Brand Partnerships Consultant
**Isabelle Friedrich McTwigan**
imctwigan@aperture.org

Advertising
**Elizabeth Morina**
emorina@aperture.org

Executive Director, Aperture
**Sarah Hermanson Meister**

**Minor White**, Editor (1952–1974)
**Michael E. Hoffman**, Publisher and Executive Director (1964–2001)
**Melissa Harris**, Editor in Chief (2002–2012)
**Chris Boot**, Executive Director (2011–2021)
**Lesley A. Martin**, Founder and Publisher, The PhotoBook Review (2011–2021)

aperture.org

Aperture is a nonprofit publisher dedicated to creating insight, community, and understanding through photography. Established in 1952 to advance "creative thinking, significantly expressed in words and photographs," Aperture champions photography's vital role in nurturing curiosity and encouraging a more just, tolerant society.

Aperture (ISSN 0003-6420) is published quarterly, in spring, summer, fall, and winter, at 548 West 28th Street, 4th Floor, New York, NY 10001. In the United States, a one-year subscription (four issues) is $75; a two-year subscription (eight issues) is $124. In Canada, a one-year subscription is $95. All other international subscriptions are $110 per year. Visit aperture.org to subscribe. Single copies may be purchased at $24.95 for most issues. Subscribe to the Aperture Digital Archive at aperture.org/archive. Periodicals postage paid at New York and additional offices. Postmaster: Send address changes to Aperture, PO Box 3000, Denville, NJ 07834. Address queries regarding subscriptions, renewals, or gifts to: Aperture Subscription Service, 866-457-4603 (US and Canada), or email custsvc_aperture@fulcoinc.com.

Newsstand distribution in the US is handled by CMG. For international distribution, contact Central Books, centralbooks.com. Other inquiries, email orders@aperture.org or call 212-505-5555.

Become a Member of Aperture to take your interest in and knowledge of photography further. With an annual tax-deductible gift of $250, membership includes a complimentary subscription to *Aperture* magazine, discounts on Aperture's award-winning publications, a special limited-edition gift, and more. To join, visit aperture.org/join, or contact membership@aperture.org.

Credits for "Curriculum," pp. 26–27: Adnan: © Stefan Ruiz; *Murder, She Wrote*: Courtesy CBS via Getty Images; *Transfigurations*: © Tarek Al-Ghoussein; Emahoy: © Tony Bogassian; *Eyes of Laura Mars*: Courtesy Columbia Pictures/Photofest

Library of Congress Catalog Card No: 58-30845.

ISBN 978-1-59711-568-1

Printed in Turkey by Ofset Yapimevi

# OFSET
## YAPIMEVİ

Support has been provided by members of Aperture's Magazine Council: Jon Stryker and Slobodan Randjelovic, Susan and Thomas Dunn, Kate Cordsen and Denis O'Leary, and Michael W. Sonnenfeldt, MUUS Collection.

**Florian W. Müller**
From the series "Singularity"
Fine Art Print on Alu-Dibond | Hahnemühle William Turner | Floater frame Basel, white matt,
19.69 x 26.38 inches | printed by WhiteWall.com

## Photography in perfection

For everyone who loves photography. For more than 15 years, artists and discerning photographers
worldwide have placed their trust in WhiteWall's photo lab. Winner of TIPA's "Best Photo Lab Worldwide",
we offer unmatched quality through the combination of traditional development and the latest
technologies. Discover our printing passion at WhiteWall.com

# Contributors

DEANA LAWSON (guest editor) is a photographer and artist based in Brooklyn and Los Angeles. Her work has been exhibited widely at such institutions as Tate Modern, MoMA PS1, the Art Institute of Chicago, the Brooklyn Museum, the Whitney Museum of American Art, and the Contemporary Art Museum St. Louis. In 2020, Lawson became the first photographer to be awarded the Solomon R. Guggenheim Museum's Hugo Boss Prize, and in 2021 her first museum survey opened at the Institute of Contemporary Art in Boston. She is a professor of visual arts at Princeton University, and is represented by Gagosian and David Kordansky Gallery. *Deana Lawson: An Aperture Monograph*, with contributions by Zadie Smith and Arthur Jafa, was published in 2018.

Sir BEN OKRI ("Impossible Truths," page 80) is an acclaimed Nigerian British poet, essayist, and novelist. He was the winner of the Booker Prize for his 1991 novel *The Famished Road*, and he was knighted in 2023 for his services to literature. Okri has published numerous books, including *An African Elegy* (1992), *Mental Fight* (1999), *Tales of Freedom* (2009), *The Age of Magic* (2014), and *A Fire in My Head* (2021). His latest novel is *The Last Gift of the Master Artists* (2023), and he recently published *Tiger Work* (2023), a collection of stories, poems, and essays about climate change.

TRACY K. SMITH ("'Tis of Thee," page 122) is a poet, memoirist, and translator. The Pulitzer Prize–winning author of five poetry collections, she served as the twenty-second poet laureate of the United States, from 2017 to 2019. Her most recent book is *To Free the Captives: A Plea for the American Soul* (2023), a personal manifesto on memory, family, and history. Smith is a professor of English and of African and African American studies at Harvard University and the Susan S. and Kenneth L. Wallach Professor at the Harvard Radcliffe Institute.

JEFF WHETSTONE's ("Field Guide to Wildflowers," page 51) photographs and films imagine America through lenses of anthropology and mythology. Trained as a biologist, Whetstone portrays the natural world in a political context and the built environment within the web of nature. His work is in the collections of the Metropolitan Museum of Art, New York Public Library, Whitney Museum of American Art, and the Yale Art Gallery, among others. Whetstone is a professor of photography and the director of the program for visual arts at Princeton University.

SIMONE WHITE ("let fani willis fuck," page 73) is the author of several collections of poetry and prose, including *House Envy of All the World* (2010), *Of Being Dispersed* (2016), *Dear Angel of Death* (2018), *or, on being the other woman* (2022), and the forthcoming *Warring*. She is an associate professor of English at the University of Pennsylvania, where she is a scholar of twentieth- and twenty-first-century Black studies and radical Black poetics.

JASON HICKEL ("Imagination," page 92) is an economic anthropologist, author, and a fellow of the Royal Society of Arts. His research focuses on global political economy, inequality, and ecological economics, which are the subjects of his two most recent books, *The Divide: A Brief Guide to Global Inequality and Its Solutions* (2017) and *Less Is More: How Degrowth Will Save the World* (2020). He is a regular contributor to *The Guardian*, *Foreign Policy*, *Jacobin*, Al Jazeera, and many other publications.

RACHEL KUSHNER ("Endnote," page 144) is a Los Angeles–based author whose novels include *Telex from Cuba* (2008), *The Flamethrowers* (2013), and *The Mars Room* (2018), which was the winner of the Prix Médicis and a finalist for the Booker Prize. Her latest books include her collection of essays *The Hard Crowd* (2021) and the novel *Creation Lake*, which was published in September. Kushner is a Guggenheim Foundation fellow and the recipient of the Harold D. Vursell Memorial Award from the American Academy of Arts and Letters.

# OWN THE MOMENT.

Discover the new Leica SL3 made in Germany.
This moment was captured by Pat Domingo.

# Paris Photo

7-10 Nov. 2024  Grand Palais

MINISTÈRE
DE LA CULTURE
*Liberté*
*Égalité*
*Fraternité*

Organised by

Official partners

# Agenda
## Exhibitions to See

### 2024 FotoFocus Biennial

Titled *backstories*, the seventh edition of FotoFocus is conceived around "stories that are not evident at first glance," satisfying desires for secret histories and deepening the art world's long archival turn. The biennial features more than one hundred photographers and eighty-three venues in Cincinnati and the region, with highlights including major presentations of work by Ansel Adams, the Columbus-raised Ming Smith, the late British Nigerian portraitist Rotimi Fani-Kayode, and Barbara Probst, best known for photographing a single instant from multiple points of view, shattering the medium's traditional frame.

2024 FotoFocus Biennial: *backstories* at venues in Greater Cincinnati, September 26–October 31, 2024

Rachael Banks, *The Wedding*, 2017
Courtesy the artist

Syd Shelton, *Darcus Howe addressing anti-racist demonstrators, Lewisham, August 13, 1977*
© Syd Shelton

### Photographing Britain

In 1980s England, a collective of musicians and activists sought to combat racism in the United Kingdom at a time when right-wing nativist groups were gaining ground. Their movement, Rock Against Racism (RAR), organized concerts and demonstrations, brought together punk and reggae acts, and highlighted the multicultural nature of British society. Syd Shelton, a photographer and designer, created a potent record of this era. His work will be included in *The 80s: Photographing Britain*, an exhibition—featuring artists from Jo Spence to Ajamu X to Martin Parr—at Tate Britain that emphasizes the vital role of collectives and artist-run publications in movements for social change.

*The 80s: Photographing Britain* at Tate Britain, London, November 21, 2024–May 5, 2025

## Sophie Calle

Stalker, stripper, thief: Sophie Calle has assumed many roles throughout her pioneering five-decade practice, which treads the "thin line there is between secret and confession," as she once put it. *Overshare*, her first survey in North America, interprets the echt-French artist's playful (and often litigious) examination of relationships—between lovers and strangers, image and text, public and private—as prescient commentary on the role of social media in shaping the self. Bringing together photographs, videos, installations, and writing, the exhibition promises to be a profound efflorescence of TMI.

*Sophie Calle: Overshare* at the Walker Art Center, Minneapolis, October 26, 2024–January 26, 2025

**Sophie Calle, *In Memory of Frank Gehry's Flowers*, 2014**
© Sophie Calle/Artists Rights Society (ARS), New York/ADAGP, Paris

## Louis Carlos Bernal

Louis Carlos Bernal was born in Arizona and began his career in the 1970s, at a time when the Chicano civil rights movement energized a generation of Mexican Americans. Bernal's revered images of homes in Tucson's historic barrios show family pictures, television sets, movie posters, and religious shrines with an exquisite attention to detail and color. "He saw his artistic mission as a kind of moral imperative, to speak for his community and to act as a bridge, to uphold his culture to the larger world," says Elizabeth Ferrer, curator of Bernal's long-awaited career retrospective. Bernal's portraits exemplify *la vida cotidiana*—everyday life—as a state of grace.

**Louis Carlos Bernal, *Los Vatos Locos, Douglas, Arizona*, 1978**
Courtesy the Center for Creative Photography, University of Arizona

*Louis Carlos Bernal: Retrospectiva* at the Center for Creative Photography, Tucson, September 14, 2024–March 15, 2025

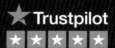

# Backstory

On Robert Frank's centennial, MoMA charts six decades of his photographs and films, including genre-bending collaborations with musicians.

**Ian Bourland**

Robert Frank spent the summer of 1972 crisscrossing America—not in pursuit of the lyrical social documentary for which he was already famed, but as part of the Rolling Stones' forty-eight-date mobile bacchanal. It had been three years since the disastrous show at the Altamont Speedway, and the band was stateside again, on the heels of a recording session in the south of France that is now etched in the annals of debauched rock excess. The tour was no exception—sex and drugs and everything else, all later mordantly recounted by Truman Capote to Andy Warhol in the pages of the magazine named for the group. The novelist registered his surprise that so much of it was unabashedly documented, that Frank was always there, camera at hand.

In many ways, the tour marked a return for Frank as well. From 1955 to 1957, he made eighty-three pictures that would be published the following year in Europe as the book *The Americans*, and republished in 1960 with an introduction by the then quintessential avatar of the road trip, Jack Kerouac. The Beat

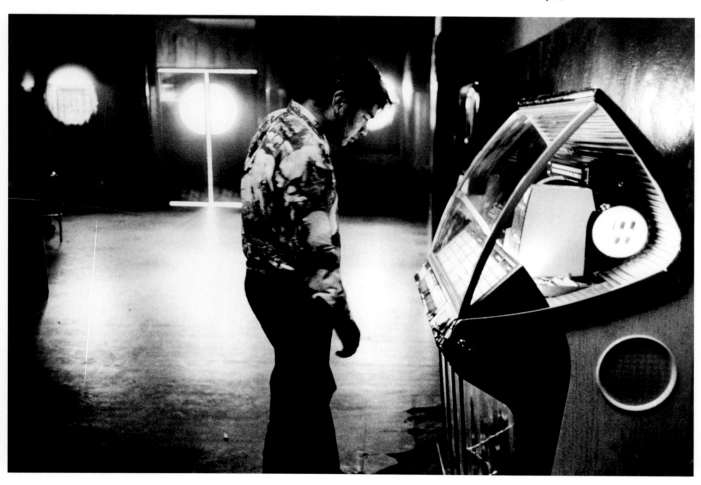

wanderer observed that a musical quality suffused Frank's frame—the Swiss-born photographer was drawn to the country's lonely jukeboxes, people swaying at roadside dives, or riders in a convertible, ablur in motion. The book encapsulated the broad humanism and compositional immediacy that drove art photography well into the 1960s, solidifying Frank's status among a younger generation (including his lifelong friend Danny Lyon) as a lodestar who chronicled a turbulent era.

The trouble with finding such success early on is that one's career is always measured against it, before and after. Ironically, the vast majority of Frank's varied output in photography, film, and performance, and his participation in the electric Lower Manhattan scene of the 1960s, happened after *The Americans*. But those genre-bending collaborations are lesser known—an imbalance that the Museum of Modern Art's current show *Life Dances On: Robert Frank in Dialogue* seeks to correct. Certainly, his episode with the Stones was but a high-profile instance of the ways in which Frank was less a lone photographer and, instead, a connector in a larger creative milieu. When he visited the band in LA, where they were wrapping *Exile on Main Street*, everyone seemed to click, and Frank was invited to shoot and design elements of the LP art (he had already captured stirring images for the mountain-folk outfit the New Lost City Ramblers) and to make an entry in the now venerable genre of auteurist concert film.

In those days, albums were events, gatefolds and liner notes scrutinized with Talmudic attention. For *Exile on Main Street*, Frank photographed the Stones in LA and New York but also interspersed older pictures, collaging and overlaying them with text. The iconic cover sequence of Arbus-esque carnival performers was actually a single image from *The Americans* rolls of the 1950s, taken from a board displayed at Hubert's Flea Circus and Museum on West 42nd Street. The photograph was already well-known by misleading titles such as *Tattoo Parlor, 8th Avenue, New York City*. As RJ Smith noted in his biography of Frank, the shifty titling foreshadowed the sort of visual remixing at play on the *Exile on Main Street* cover and throughout the photographer's career. Frank seemed keen to dirty up his image before it settled into hagiography, letting the

**Still from *Summer Cannibals*, 1996. Four minutes, six seconds, black and white, sound**
All images courtesy the Museum of Modern Art, New York; the June Leaf and Robert Frank Foundation; and Pace Gallery

Musicians liked Frank because he turned a sympathetic eye to the margins of the American experience.

meaning of his pictures drift by putting them in new contexts.

Musicians liked Frank because he turned a sympathetic eye to the margins of the American experience, foregrounding its grubbier contours. Although much of his later life was spent in the artists' enclave of Cape Breton, Nova Scotia (alongside Joan Jonas, Richard Serra, and JoAnne Akalaitis), Frank always kept one foot in the Bowery, often turning up at haunts such as CBGB, where he met Patti Smith. The photojournalist Ted Barron recalls stumbling upon him in Tompkins Square Park one day in 1985, crouched on the pavement to capture a dashingly coiffed Tom Waits in conjunction with the *Rain Dogs* album. Waits was then cast in Frank's 1987 feature made with Rudy Wurlitzer, *Candy Mountain*, about another road trip—a quest to Nova Scotia in search of a reclusive guitar luthier.

That sort of recurrence of old acquaintances in new guises is a common thread in Frank's many projects over the years. He met the British actor David Warrilow in 1975, and cast him in the full-color music video for New Order's lesser-known 1989 track "Run." More striking still was Frank's collaboration with Smith on the music video for her 1996 song "Summer Cannibals." Here, the roving lens and warped angles developed in his earlier stills inform his cinematic approach: they made Frank's style feel newly fresh, and also of a piece with a host of black-and-white videos emblematic of the form's maturation during the early 1990s. Both projects were typical examples of reinvention through tuning into the frequencies of other creators. In this way, the MoMA show reminds us that the shopworn tale of the solitary genius artist is rarely true: those icons always get by with a little help from their friends.

Ian Bourland writes on art and pop culture and is the author of *Bloodflowers: Rotimi Fani-Kayode, Photography, and the 1980s* (2019).

# As artists let's not just look at the world, let's look after it

At Skink Ink we believe climate stability to be
the most pressing issue of our time. If we all
play our part, humanity can survive.

We pride ourselves on being green.

Our inks are water based.
We use no chemicals.
Our papers are made with renewable fibers,
from agave to hemp, mulberry and bamboo.
Our cotton papers are often made with waste lint
from clothing manufacturers. In our studio we
recycle all of our papers, packing materials
and retired electronics.

There is still much to do

# Make (sustainable) Prints

## Skink Ink Fine Art Printing

Edition & Exhibition Printmakers
For Artists & Photographers

Tel: 646 455 3400 | Email: Services@skink.ink | Web: Skink.ink

# Viewfinder
## Legacy Russell parses the racial codes of American visual culture.

**Tiana Reid**

I Sell the Shadow to Support the Substance.
SOJOURNER TRUTH.

Thirty-three years ago, a man in Los Angeles named George Holliday used his new camcorder to film what would come to be known as the Rodney King tape. In 1993, the Whitney Biennial looped the entire ten-minute clip at the entrance to the exhibition, relegating King to the unwitting star of a white man's art project. In 2020, amid the international wave of uprisings after the hypervisible murders of Black people at the hands of the police, Holliday attempted to auction the camera he used to record the footage with a starting bid of

$225,000. By that time, King himself had been dead for eight years, having drowned, at the age of forty-seven, in his swimming pool on Father's Day in 2012. This abysmal chronology begs the question: How was the virality of Black death, and its attendant profit-making apparatus, set in motion long before the arrival of social media?

The curator and writer Legacy Russell devotes a chapter to King in her new book, *Black Meme: A History of the Images That Make Us* (2024), a citationally dexterous, centuries-spanning account of the racial codes that constitute US visual culture told through analyses of film, internet spectacle, contemporary art, political economy, algorithms, and more. Largely associated with online humor and trends, the meme is here historicized as a technology indexing anti-Black violence, as exemplified by Mamie Till-Mobley's decision to widely circulate graphic, open-casket images of her son, Emmett, who was murdered while visiting family in Mississippi in 1955. "Let the people see what they did to my boy," she said of her choice to publish the photographs in *Jet* magazine. This example is juxtaposed with the controversy around Dana Schutz's *Open Casket*, her 2016 painting based on those same images of Emmett Till's body. That year, George Zimmerman claims to have sold the gun he used to kill Trayvon Martin for a quarter of a million dollars. Lynching postcards are available on eBay right this minute. *Black Meme* demonstrates how digital culture relies on not only the sale of Blackness but also capitalist speculation.

Russell toggles between the narrating of facts and events and a call to arms reminiscent of her first book, *Glitch Feminism: A Manifesto* (2020), which recuperates digital errors (static, feedback, viruses, et cetera) as tools for cyberfeminist liberation. A rejection of the seamless and the stable, the book exposes how contemporary society, with its heteronormativities and exploitations, is already a malfunction. *Black Meme*'s polemic is smaller scale, maybe even counterintuitive. If the Black meme is a trope (a figure that circulates, a rhetorical device) and a trap (a deception, an injunction, an image inseparable from property and white spectatorship), Russell's response is a reading practice that requires one to "consider with slowness," interrupting the breakneck pace of the digital.

Many images in *Black Meme*—such as David Hammons's tattered American/Pan-African flag in *Oh say can you see* (2017); Lauren Halsey's 2023 rooftop installation for the Metropolitan Museum of Art, *the eastside of south central los angeles hieroglyph prototype architecture (I)*; and Amy Sherald's 2020 aquamarine portrait of Breonna Taylor—go unmentioned in the essay; they're deployed not as illustrations but to create a "montage and disruption inside the text itself." The first of twenty-one color plates is a still from Aria Dean's video *Eulogy for a Black Mass* (2017), in which the artist examines how memes mimic the dialectical tensions of Blackness—ubiquitous and disregarded, enjoyed and devalued—over a compilation of Vine, YouTube, and Instagram videos made by Black creators.

Russell's book offers a "study of the prehistory of the internet" as she reevaluates nineteenth- and twentieth-century art, film, and media through the lens of contemporary cyberculture. She contends that Sojourner Truth's iconic 1864 carte-de-visite portrait, captioned "I Sell the Shadow to Support the Substance," belongs to a long history of Black memes that reveals entanglements of property, image making, and autonomy. The unreleased, Black-cast, 1913 film *Lime Kiln Field Day* stars Bert Williams and Odessa Warren Grey, who kiss on screen. Russell sets this rare, early record of intimacy between two Black people in conversation with Garrett Bradley's 2019 experimental short *America*, which repurposes footage from *Lime Kiln Field Day*. Bradley explains that behind her film's generic title was a desire to repopulate search engines so that "America," resignified through Black visual culture,

Top:
**Aria Dean, Still from**
***Eulogy for a Black Mass*,**
**2017; bottom: T. Hayes**
**Hunter and Edwin**
**Middleton, Still from**
***Lime Kiln Field Day*, 1913**
Dean: Courtesy the artist;
Hunter and Middleton; ©
The Museum of Modern
Art/SCALA/Art Resource,
NY

*Black Meme* offers a "study of the prehistory of the internet."

could be embodied by a Black kiss and not white-supremacist images like those in D. W. Griffith's *The Birth of a Nation*, which was released two years after *Lime Kiln Field Day* and helped revive the Ku Klux Klan.

"Memetic Blackness" is the term that Russell uses to describe how Blackness, as material, gets copied and transmitted in an ouroboric loop. "Blackness *in itself* is memetic," she argues. "The technology of memes as a core component of a dawning of digital culture has been driven by, shaped by, authored by, Blackness." Russell makes plain that the internet did not inaugurate a fixation on racist images, iconography, and symbols, though it likely does, as she puts it, "accelerate the density of their circulation."

Russell sometimes dilutes her argument by gathering so many nodes of Black history into her framework; she describes a 1965 Selma to Montgomery civil rights march as "an example of a pre-internet, media-generated 'flash mob'" and suggests that "the first Black memes were those transmitted via the Middle Passage," inasmuch that Black people were themselves forms of data forcibly migrating along a route similar to that of transatlantic communication cables. While at times this revisionism feels like a stretch, so much of Blackness is malleable, fungible, and instrumental. Blackness *does* stretch, and it gets stretched so far that it tears.

**Tiana Reid is a writer and
an assistant professor of
English at York University
in Toronto.**

**Exhibition**

# ICONIC NATURE PHOTOGRAPHS

## *A Collection of American Vintage Prints*

### 15th September 2024 to 29th March 2025

Steichen  Cunningham  Weston  Strand  Adams  Lavenson  Bullock  Bernhard
Van Dyke  White  Baer  Byers  Gilpin  Worth  DeCosse  Caponigro  Giles
Tice  Kolbrener  Wimberley  Mapplethorpe  Werling  Witherill
Nixon  Sexton  Loranc  Maddox ...

For
Collectors
Museums
Visitors

**WBB GALLERY**
www.wbb.gallery
Zurich

# Redux

## Rafael Goldchain captured tender moments against a backdrop of political violence in Latin America.

**Yxta Maya Murray**

Over the last decade, the Art Gallery of Ontario embarked on an initiative to incorporate twentieth-century photography detailing life in Argentina, Chile, Nicaragua, Honduras, Guatemala, El Salvador, and Mexico into its collections. Beyond poetic images created by Graciela Iturbide and Manuel Álvarez Bravo, the Toronto museum also houses photographs of protests and coups. Such grim subjects might be expected in a Latin American collection: during the latter half of the century, the region was convulsed by civil wars, a genocide, dictatorship, and murderous US intervention.

One recent acquisition provides an unexpected twist: lushly colored images by Rafael Goldchain, a Chilean-born photographer of Polish Jewish heritage, who settled in Toronto in the 1970s and in the mid-1980s traveled on a grant to Mexico and Central America. There, he took pictures of residents who struggled on the sidelines of the Guatemalan civil war, CIA interference in Honduras, and Nicaragua's revolution. Yet instead of focusing on conflict's "decisive moments," Goldchain showed lyrical glimpses of people's desire, grief, repose, and piety.

Such is the case in *A Young Man's Grave, Nicaragua* (1986), which reveals a collage adorning a final resting place. The artwork frames a studio portrait of the deceased, a wide-eyed, thinly mustachioed stripling surrounded by dried flowers, clouds, and angels. The offering is saturated with intense blues. "I was in a cemetery in Matagalpa," Goldchain told me recently, mentioning the city in west-central Nicaragua involved in the Iran–Contra conflict. "Had this young man fallen as part of that? I didn't know. I had heard that there was a tradition where children who pass away automatically become angels. This boy was of the age that he could be both, a soldier and an angel."

Goldchain's ability to freeze tender, ambiguous moments against the backdrop of political violence constitutes a distinct kind of conflict photography. The 1980s "were the era of Susan Sontag and the whole Goya perception of pain," AGO curator Marina Dumont-Gauthier explained. She referenced Sontag's *On Photography* (1977), which inveighs against the power of war images to anesthetize viewers to suffering. "What Rafael is offering is so different," she said. According to Dumont-Gauthier, back when Goldchain photographed his images, people were not ready to view complex and polysemous images of war "because it somehow felt disingenuous." She thinks the time is now ripe for Goldchain's approach. "The pain is still there. Once the war is over, these stories continue."

Goldchain presents the continuing story in works such as *Easter Procession, Santiago Atitlán, Guatemala* (1986). Depicting ten men carrying a tinseled casket that appears to contain a statue of Jesus Christ in the tradition of Santa Semana, the picture achieves a forward propulsion amplified by the undulating line created by the heads and shoulders of the pallbearers. The image's mingling of beauty and mourning is complicated by the fact that four years after it was taken, army soldiers would open fire on an unarmed crowd of Tz'utujil Mayans in Santiago Atitlán as part of the atrocities that punctuated the country's civil war.

"I wasn't a war photographer," Goldchain told me. "I sometimes took photos of bullets in walls, semi-destroyed ruins, but those pictures didn't have any of the complexity that I was after. And I didn't want a bullet in the heart either. My work is more elliptical."

Goldchain's allusive impulses led to *Nocturnal Encounter, Comayagua, Honduras* (1987), which initially reads like a snapshot of carefree lovers. A man wearing a striped blue shirt smiles down at a dark-haired woman who sways her hips. The innocent-looking assignation takes place in a turquoise-and-cerulean alleyway. But knowledge of the political context introduces menacing undertones of male dominance to the photograph. "During the Iran–Contra affair, there was a very large air base in Honduras called Palmerola. There were a lot of bars where American soldiers met lovely Honduran girls. This is a red-light district, a meat market."

"Rafael's work allows people to engage with photography that tells a fuller story," Dumont-Gauthier said, an affirmation of Goldchain's Mexican and Central American images that resonates with the recent institutional validation of Latinx photographers, such as Louis Carlos Bernal and Paz Errázuriz, who breathed new life into the documentary tradition in the 1970s and 1980s. The curator also noted Goldchain's deliberate use of color, suggesting that "Blue is associated with nostalgia. The colors help us process our own emotions. If the photo were against a red backdrop,

Previous page: *Nocturnal Encounter, Comayagua, Honduras, 1987*; this spread, clockwise from top right: *A Tehuantepec Maiden, Juchitán, Oaxaca, México, 1986*; *Easter Procession, Santiago Atitlán, Guatemala, 1986*; *A Young Man's Grave, Nicaragua, 1986*
Courtesy the artist

"I wasn't a war photographer," Goldchain said. "My work is more elliptical."

it would have a completely different meaning."

Goldchain's associative palette perhaps finds its deepest expression in *A Tehuantepec Maiden, Juchitán, Oaxaca, México* (1986), where a girl wearing a huipil stitched with crimson-and-pink florals stands against a mural of the Virgin of Guadalupe. As in *A Young Man's Grave, Nicaragua*, a painted sky forms the backdrop. The jaunty artificial flowers in the girl's hair contrast with her stoic expression. Does her steadfast look telegraph the larger struggle of armed forces disappearing and murdering Oaxacan dissidents during this era? The girl's gaze seems almost unnervingly grave in light of that history.

"She was fifteen years old," Goldchain recalled, nodding his head contemplatively. "When I first showed these photos, people said I was noncommittal and too artistic and aesthetic. But I could only be who I could be."

Yxta Maya Murray is a regular contributor to *Aperture*.

# Dispatches
## In India's seaside town of Panjim, an archival project conjures Goa's cosmopolitan past.

Lola Mac Dougall

Grandpa wearing his best Sunday suit, the second cousin's first communion, the aunt who made it big as a singer in Bollywood, a family member whose name nobody can ever remember in costume at the carnival parade, the uncle who moved to Brazil never to return but kept sending gifts and photographs. These are some of the images one may encounter in Goa Familia, an archive documenting family histories through vernacular photography, with highlights presented as an installation each year in Panjim, Goa's capital.

Last December, I visited its third edition, curated by Akshay Mahajan and Lina Vincent and titled *Let the Sound Linger*, hinting at the potential of both songs and photographs to remain in one's mind

well after being heard or seen. There were few original prints—perhaps they were too fragile to make the trip from their domestic environments to the exhibition space, in the old Goa Medical College—and the reproductions presented in the show were left intentionally raw, showing, on occasion, frayed borders, moth stains, or even cracks. The care of family photographs has traditionally been assigned to women, and the act of preserving them in a charged tropical environment like that of Goa, with four monsoon months and extremely high humidity, is almost heroic.

Goa was Portugal's first territorial possession in Asia (Afonso de Albuquerque reached its shores in 1510), and it subsequently became the capital of its

eastern empire. This unique geopolitical position resulted in a cosmopolitanism still felt today and discernible in its photographic traces. Many viewers first became acquainted with Goan homes thanks to Prabuddha Dasgupta's book *Edge of Faith* (2009), which explores the state's Catholic community, as well as from the evocative, open-ended photographic projects of Dayanita Singh, whose photoshoots in Saligao, the village where she has resided part-time for over two decades, imbue household objects with auratic interiority. In both bodies of work, possessions exude a certain worldliness: a bone china tea set from Macao, a Ugandan gazelle antler presiding over the living room, and a hand-painted Portuguese tile inscribed with a Lusophone-sounding family name suggest the layered stories behind Goa's material wealth.

As the writer Vivek Menezes describes in the 2015 catalog for the festival GoaPhoto, photography was sought after as much by the Goan middle class of the second half of the nineteenth century as by its European counterparts. These families attempted to "commemorate their own gentrification" and appear "comfortably poised between East and West, ready to absorb whatever modernity would bring," he writes. In 1843, it was decided that Panjim would become Goa's capital and be remodeled along the lines of Lisbon's historic downtown, with a grid of streets parallel and perpendicular to the Mandovi River.

*Families Are Like Rivers*, the title of Goa Familia's 2022 exhibition, highlighted the importance of this river and its promenade, which offered strollers the perfect backdrop to flaunt their hybrid identities. That year, the main exhibition space consisted of a photo collage—an homage to Ed Ruscha's *Every Building on the Sunset Strip* (1966)—where a contemporary view of the edifices along the riverfront was overlaid with archival images, including examples from the photo-albums of the very families who once inhabited these buildings or ran businesses from their premises. It was a compelling juggling of opposing forces: the rootedness of the photo-album versus the dislocation of the Goan diaspora.

Through the collage, the images were given a second life, this time a public viewing. In one photograph, a young

Opposite:
**Akshay Mahajan, *Families Are Like Rivers*, 2022;** this page, top: Installation view of the exhibition *Goa Familia*, 2019; bottom: Costume party at Clube Nacional, Panjim, Goa, n.d. Courtesy the artist, Fatima Lobato de Faria Alvares, and Serendipity Arts Foundation

man named Carmo Fernandes reclines on a balustrade, Brownie camera dangling from his hand. Photographed in black and white in 1960, just a year before the end of Portuguese colonial rule, he epitomizes the riverside promenade etiquette: to nonchalantly stroll up and down while observing and being observed. The snapshot has been patched into a color photograph taken at the same exact coordinates today. If a specific use of the colonial archive was to forcefully administrate the border between past and present, the family album inhabits a more porous understanding of time, this mise en abyme suggests. Poised between epochs, the young man becomes a memory while holding our gaze in the here and now.

The next edition of Goa Familia will open on December 15, 2024, as part of the Serendipity Arts Festival.

Lola Mac Dougall is a Spanish curator and writer based in Goa. She is a cofounder of GoaPhoto and JaipurPhoto.

# Curriculum
## Farah Al Qasimi

Farah Al Qasimi describes her aesthetic as "so-much-ness." Inspired by everything from *SpongeBob SquarePants* to Octavia Butler's dystopian novels, the Emirati-raised maximalist tends toward extravagant ornamentation and sly obfuscation in her photographs, which filter consumer culture, futurist kitsch, and the trappings of femininity through a dizzying postcolonial lens to examine how images shape desire on both global and intimate scales.

### THE ARAB APOCALYPSE
I don't think there's anything I can say about Etel Adnan's book-length poem *The Arab Apocalypse* (1989) that will do it any justice. It's riotous, haunting, and visually rich. When I read it, the voice in my head wants to scream.

### MURDER, SHE WROTE
Hear me out. *MSW* is one of those shows that's easy to turn a nose up at, because it's always on. My mother has loved watching it for years, and I only recently caught on. It's funny, the outfits are great, and I can never guess who the culprit is.

### TRANSFIGURATIONS
Tarek Al-Ghoussein's *Transfigurations* (2014) is a beautiful and quiet series of photographs pondering displacement and one's relationship to a physical land. The images follow a simple script—they are mostly self-portraits with a figure and a ground—yet there is something new to discover in each of them. Al-Ghoussein was a Palestinian Kuwaiti artist and educator, and a dear friend to many. His legacy of presence and thoughtfulness lives on through his work.

See page 6 for image credits.

## EMAHOY TSEGUÉ-MARYAM GUÈBROU

Emahoy Tsegué-Maryam Guèbrou is one of my favorite composers and pianists. Her rhythm is complex and expressive, and her songs feel like the result of being someone deeply attentive to the world around them. I listen to the 2016 Emahoy compilation album a lot when I go home to the UAE, driving past the sand dunes at night, imagining spirits dancing somewhere in the dark.

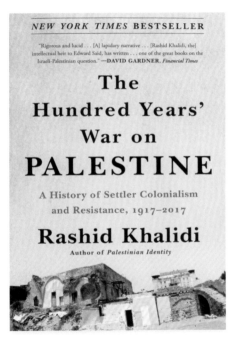

## RASHID KHALIDI

Rashid Khalidi's book *The Hundred Years' War on Palestine* (2020) is an important introductory history of the Palestinian struggle since the Balfour Declaration and essential reading for anyone who would like to expand their understanding of the region in this current moment.

## EYES OF LAURA MARS

In this 1978 American *giallo*, Faye Dunaway stars as a celebrity fashion photographer who has a psychic connection with a serial killer. I love horror and thriller films—they're a way to exorcise fear and anxiety consciously, rather than letting them sit dormant. I don't know how logical this hypothesis is, but *Eyes of Laura Mars* is a great film. And there's something comical about Hollywood's portrayal of a photographic career (of course, this was the 1970s, when print media was thriving and photographers were paid a livable project rate). Her apartment is styled beautifully, and Barbra Streisand belts out a dramatic theme song.

# Preview

## High above San Francisco Bay, Richard Misrach creates a sublime but eerie vision of global trade.

**Brian Dillon**

"Nor breath nor motion"—the container ships in these photographs by Richard Misrach have the deathly stillness of the becalmed vessel in Samuel Taylor Coleridge's *The Rime of the Ancient Mariner*, stuck "As idle as a painted ship. / Upon a painted ocean." On the one hand, here are seascapes of benign sublimity, silver light and grisaille clouds, golden dawns and jewel lights reflected in a smoked-glass sea. A scale and spectacle that Misrach has long embraced in his work, knowingly courting a Romanticism just on the edge of kitschy vacancy. But then there are the ships, ranged in San Francisco Bay, seemingly rooted in this leaden expanse like artificial islands or menacing fortresses. In *Cargo Ships* (2021–ongoing), begun during the COVID epidemic, the stranded freighters look like monuments —but to what?

In 1997, Misrach moved into a house in the Berkeley Hills overlooking the bay; he could see the north shore of San Francisco, the empty Alcatraz prison island, the Golden Gate Bridge. From this

vantage, he took thousands of photographs: in sequence, they would compose an abrupt cinema of light and weather, unfolding around bridge and prison and sailing boats. (These images are something like the opposite of Hiroshi Sugimoto's celebrated seascapes, which frame inscrutable gray horizons from shores around the world.) With *Cargo Ships*, Misrach repeats the iterations of his *Golden Gate* pictures, but this time the world has stalled, or at least slowed, with him.

The Port of Oakland, for which the ships were bound when Misrach made around two thousand pictures of them, was in 1962 the first major port on the Pacific coast of the United States to be refitted for container traffic. Today, it moves 99 percent of Northern California's containerized goods; about three-quarters of its trade is with Asia. These are the goods and vessels we see backed up in the bay in Misrach's photographs, which he took not from his home, as before, but at an undisclosed

*Cargo Ships (December 03, 2023 7:41 am)*, 2023

*Cargo Ships* alludes to a long history of the marine picturesque in art, but also to darker disruptions.

location nearby. It is 2021, and although international trade has recovered from the delays at the height of the pandemic, ports like Oakland's are still affected by workforce illness. If one of the consequences of COVID was that global logistics, at the moment of its failure, suddenly became visible, *Cargo Ships* also essays a more abstracted or conceptual monument to a time of disaster for some and of continued (if constrained) consumption for others.

*Cargo Ships* is not the first series of Misrach's to fathom catastrophe. While his photographs of deserts and oceans— with sparse and tiny human figures, as if for scale in some eighteenth-century geological engraving—often point subtly to encounters between environment and humanity, he has also produced more direct and punctual images of their effects on each other. In 1991, after fire decimated the Oakland-Berkeley area, killing twenty-five people and consuming more than three thousand homes, Misrach photographed burnt-out houses,

*Cargo Ships (November 14, 2023 6:56 am)*, 2023
Courtesy the artist; Pace Gallery, New York; Fraenkel Gallery, San Francisco; and Mark Selwyn Fine Art, Los Angeles

a melted plastic tricycle, a swimming pool surrounded by baked wreckage. (Misrach waited until the fire's twentieth anniversary before exhibiting these pictures.) In 2005, in the wake of Katrina, he traveled to New Orleans and took digital images of post-hurricane graffiti: "Help! Help!," "Resign Bush," "Michael where are you?"

Assuredly, *Cargo Ships* alludes to a long history of the marine picturesque in art, but also to darker disruptions: crowded naval battle scenes in Dutch painting, shipwrecks and the extremity of Théodore Géricault's *The Raft of the Medusa*, the way light and mood and water in J. M. W. Turner may turn chaotic or mournful. Before the pandemic, Misrach was already planning, with the art historian Tyler Green, a book related to the history of art and seafaring, for which he had been photographing a yacht wrecked in Hawaii. Regarding his landmark documentary and conceptual project *Fish Story* (1989–95), Allan Sekula said that part of the point was simply to

remind us that the ocean exists as an economic, political, technologized entity. In an era of trade interrupted by piracy and pandemic, in a period of mass migration (and mass death) by sea, Misrach's photographs are a comparable reminder —more ambiguous, more frankly aesthetic, no less timely.

Brian Dillon is currently working on a book about Kate Bush and another on aesthetic education.

# Interview

## Emmet Gowin has been sorting through decades of photographs, discovering unseen images and memories.

**Rebecca Bengal**

Emmet Gowin came to photography via a teenage revelation in a dentist's office in Danville, Virginia. It was the late 1950s. Flipping through magazines in the waiting room, the minister's son landed on an Ansel Adams photograph of a burned tree stump sprouting fresh shoots. Out loud, he exclaimed, "Oh my goodness, this is the Christ." Now, Gowin says, "Thank God nobody else was there. But to me, it was clear. This was the transformation of death into life." He went home and asked to borrow the family camera.

Gowin would first become known for his stunningly open and intimate photographs of his wife, Edith, and her extended family in 1960s and 1970s rural Virginia, pictures Robert Adams has described as "a lovely testament of close-in wonder and affection." While Gowin cites Harry Callahan and Frederick Sommer as guiding influences, of his wife, he claims: "I was already a full version of me when I met Edith, but I am ten times me because of her." In the 1980s, Gowin's scope shifted and grew concentrically outward, focusing on environmental devastation—both natural, as in the case of Mount St. Helens, or by human hand, as with the Nevada test sites for atomic weapons. Other series, on colorful nocturnal moths and forests in Central and South America, explore the marvels of biodiversity.

It is possible to think of Gowin's early pictures, and the nuclear sites that occupied his consciousness long before he was able to photograph them, as metaphors for light and shadow: "Emmet Gowin is an artist who bears witness to wholeness in beauty and violence. He understands that one cannot exist without the other," wrote his friend Terry Tempest Williams.

Princeton University, where Gowin is professor emeritus, recently announced that its art museum will acquire Gowin's archive, which includes more than six hundred fifty photographs (and will continue to grow as he makes new work), some seven thousand contact sheets, negatives, book maquettes, and correspondence. Recently, I spoke with Gowin from his home in Pennsylvania.

Rebecca Bengal: **You've been through various periods of reflection when it comes to curating major retrospective exhibitions of your work. How is this time different? What kind of**

**discoveries do you make when revisiting your pictures as an archive?**

**Emmet Gowin**: I had a trick in class when it was the day to make the first print: each student would choose an image from a film roll we'd made together, and that was their print. Meanwhile, I'd always go through my own material and find something I made at their age—not terribly special, just interesting enough to print. Sometimes, once the print was made, I would realize, Oh, it's much more than I expected. The poet Wendell

Berry says that good work, after it's done, takes yet more time to prove its worth, and you're not really in charge. You're not the final arbiter of that.

Even before organizing the archive, it was the pandemic period that really turned me into a student of my own work. I started over again, at the beginning. I had a lot of time, and I began to print things I'd tried to print when I was young but didn't have the skill. I was looking back at the innocent family backyard pictures that we made all our lives. They weren't quite super art,

but they're the real, intimate, nuanced moments.

RB: **Super art?**

**EG**: Well, "super art" is a kind of short-hand. In many ways, I think our task as human beings all boils down to what we do every day. It's what you do every day that counts. You go through days of simple activities, finding an old print, and refining it somehow, or just reminding yourself that it's worth more time and attention. It's really little increments of behavior that form a kind of aesthetic life. We get a sense of who we are by the way we treat the most ordinary things.

When I unfold a word, or a concept like super art, I'm contrasting the responsibility we hold on to every day, to the life and meaning and fulfillment that you take. I ran out first thing this morning before coffee to check on my little peony that I grafted last fall, and its little leaves are coming up out of the ground. And I'm so exhilarated and thrilled with that process that the day brings me joy. That's very analogous to the artist's life as I have experienced it. You just do the things you do as well as you can, and then, you get out of the way.

RB: **I want to pose a question to you that you raised in a talk you gave in 2013. You said: "What is that quality of intimacy that we love in a picture?"**

EG: You know, I was drifting into the crowd after that talk when an older man rushed up to me and asked, "Why are you the way you are?" I thought, Wow, that's not just a bold question, that's an impertinent question. But what I said was, "It's very simple. I think it's because I always wanted to be just like my mother." I think intimacy is what you cannot tell your mother. It's what your mother already knows. From the moment we were married, Edith and I made the conscious decision that we would not show the pictures we were making to my parents. That was our intimacy. What I could barely talk about to anyone somehow comes out in a picture. That is what intimacy amounts to in images. It's something that you can barely speak of, and yet, it's the most important thing in the world.

RB: **That reminds me of a photograph of yours, one of Edith when you're visiting her relatives in Virginia, where, just out of sight of her family, she flashes open her top to the camera.**

EG: There was also a version where we were at her great-grandmother's house, and, while rocking back and forth, her great-grandmother was in this rhythm of asking questions, as she dipped snuff. Edith's impulse and the great-grandmother's leaning forward to spit the snuff into a can were in synchronicity, and there was the picture. One evening, Edith was in her mother's bedroom, taking a kind of simple bath from a pan of hot water on the stove. She'd gotten herself naked and was washing off with a washcloth, and I got my 16mm film camera. I'm sitting on the floor filming, when her mother walked in, took one look at the two of us, and says, "This is the right room. I've just picked the wrong moment."

RB: **Can you put into words what it is that you see in those moments when you ask Edith to stay as she is for a picture?**

I had a lot of time, and I began to print things I'd tried to print when I was young but didn't have the skill.

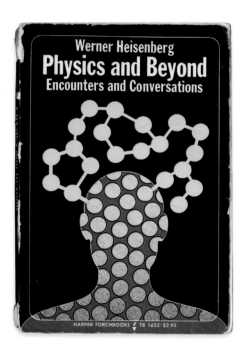

EG: I think about a picture I made of her from '72, '73, where she's standing in a doorway. I remember asking her to, maybe, lift her arm just a little bit, some innocuous thing, and looking into the camera and feeling, This is as close to living perfection as I'm ever going to be. And she can't hold this forever. She owns it, but it's only ours for a little while. That struck me that day so powerfully. You're always on the edge of that. Anything worthwhile is, in a way, something you'll never see again.

RB: **You've said before that the family pictures, the backyard images, are also, in their own way, war pictures.**

EG: During the first week of graduate school, in 1965, I got a letter from the draft board saying to report to active duty. And it was during that trip to the board in Danville that I made a picture, at the behest of my niece, of her lying on the ground surrounded by her dolls. Harry Callahan called it my first photograph. He sensed that it wasn't a picture about other pictures, but that it was a picture of the beating heart of life itself.

Our lives were in a kind of bracket surrounded by the Vietnam War, and our lives were conditioned by the war. It was made all the more vivid because the war was going on, and we knew we were not participating in it directly, but it affected everything in everybody's life. It was the background against which those pictures happened.

RB: **What prompted you to turn outward, to photograph beyond those intimate family pictures?**

EG: Well, the world changes, and you change. There was a point when the patriarchs and matriarchs in Edith's family started to die. I realized, Oh, I get the lesson of this. You can't have the same subject your whole life.

In the 1980s, I was reading a lot of physics and a lot of Native American literature in which they refer to the awareness of "the long body." The shaman would give instructions to the novitiate who's getting ready to go up into the mountains for the vision quest, to fast and pray and wait for the vision to come—the awareness of how you started your life, and who you are now, and what you will be at the end of your life, in your

Top:
Spread from *Hidden Likeness* (2015);
bottom: *Nancy, 1965*

imagination. The idea is that you live consciously aware of the continuum even though you're in the moment. It embodies the day that Crazy Horse faced Custer; as the Lakota Sioux were leaving the village, they supposedly said to each other, "What a day to die." What a consciousness of the beauty of the day I have in me now. Therefore, I can go to uncertainty.

**RB: If war is subtext in your early family pictures, it becomes more visible, even eerie, in bodies of work such** as the *Nevada Test Site* **photographs (1996–97).**

**EG:** That work began when I was able to photograph the Hanford Nuclear Reservation, where the plutonium for the first atomic bombs was "made." When I first visited, it happened to be a rainy, gray, dark, ominous day. But as we flew over the site, for a minute, the sun came out, and it was like a feeling of forgiveness just swept over that awful place. And I thought, That's right. The sun doesn't care. The sun is not having thoughts

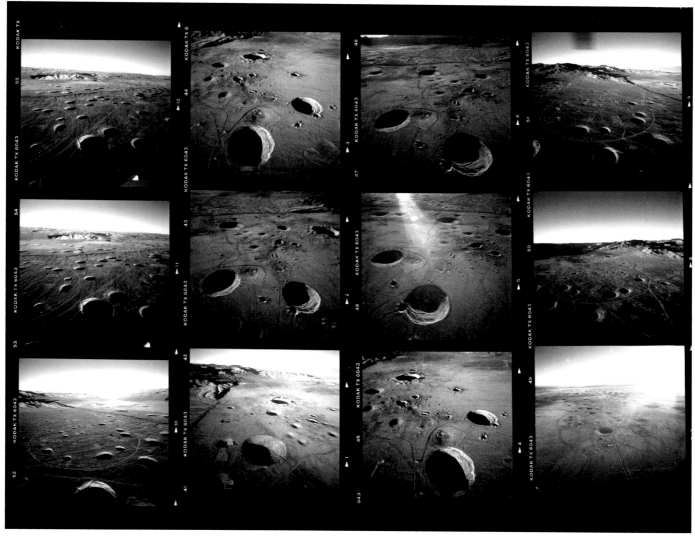

**Contact print for *The Nevada Test Site*, 1996**
Unless noted, all images courtesy the artist

about thermonuclear reactions. In fact, it *is* one. Immediately, I started wondering, What does the landscape look like where the bombs were tested?

RB: **Your next project, *Mariposas Nocturnas* (1997–2015), is radically different in scope, embracing ecology, color, life. How consciously did that come about?**

EG: I had gone with friends to Ecuador in 1997. I had always been interested in insects and nature in every manifestation, and my department chairman had found someone who would take us out in the forest and show us how to collect insects. Immediately, I felt the transposition of my feelings between the test site and being in the tropical forest: the smell of the forest and the wetness and the fear of it. It just seemed so exquisitely wonderful. I didn't care if I ever went

back to the test site again, though I actually would.

It liberated me to change direction. I was making a bit of a jump, but I had always felt that the transition from the family as subject to the rest was, in a way, a natural one. For me, the subject is just wherever the family occurs, the awareness of how we fit into the places around us, how we belong to the Earth. We went to England and to Ireland, to Italy, to the Czech Republic, to Jordan, to Granada. And I just kept at it.

Rebecca Bengal is the author of *Strange Hours: Photography, Memory, and the Lives of Artists* (Aperture, 2023).

# Arrhythmic Mythic Ra

# Guest Editor's Note
## Deana Lawson

For captions and credits, see page 125.

It seems the photographs that I'm most drawn to in my conscious looking life push against our preconceived notions of social and aesthetic norms, images that are abrasive to our tastes, that make our model of the world more complicated. Photography, the outlier, is most adept at reminding us of instability and fallibilities. I believe we all need to observe things we don't understand. And as someone who makes pictures, I'm reminded that a photograph, by its nature, can deliver more about the subject than even the photographer or the subject intend. With this in mind, I have arranged a constellation of images that operate like texts and texts that operate like pictures—fragmented, arrhythmic, mythic.

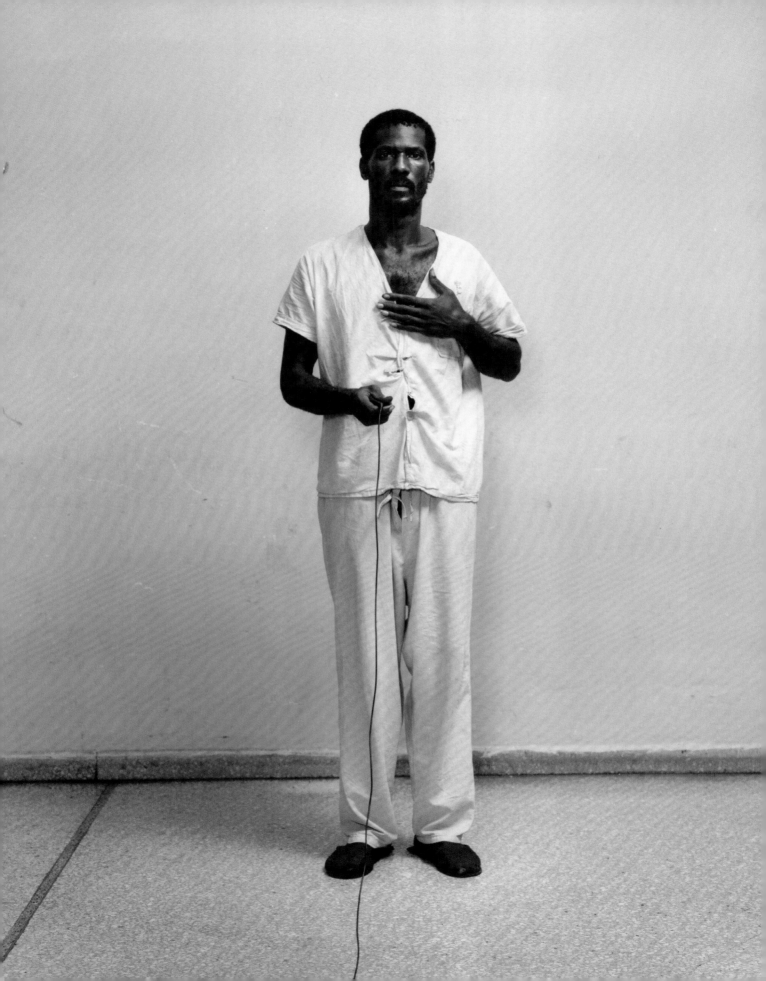

# Field Guide to Wildflowers

Jeff Whetstone

River Road descended from soybean fields into swampland on the drive to Jude's house. The covered dish rode shotgun. I went under the speed limit to avoid any jostling since I had plated the portions so carefully, arranging all of Jude's favorite foods in a spiral pattern. Corn pie, butter beans, red rice, and turkey breast formed the petals. For the center, I set three bright lemon twists in a bold red dollop of cranberry sauce like a pistil and stigma. The whole dish looked like a blossom. I knew my cousin would appreciate it. He was a botanist. A professor emeritus of botany.

Black water mirrored the sunset through cypress trees. I didn't come back here often enough. In my youth, my hunter uncles had taught me how to read the codes written into the South Carolina landscape by its wild game. I never took up the sport. Jude was the only man I knew around here who taught me there was something to look for in these woods besides trophies.

I knocked on his porch door, balancing the warm plate on one palm, and stood back ready to unveil my creation to Jude; instead, Jimmie opened the door.

"I thought I would bring Jude a plate," I said in my holiday-glad voice. I added, in a minor key, "If I knew you were here, I would have brought you a plate too."

"Well, that is awful kind of you." He seemed startled, like he just woke up. I wasn't sure if he remembered it was Thanksgiving.

Jimmie slicked his black hair into place and slinked onto the porch, closing the door behind him. His belt cinched his pants tight to his tiny waist. His lips were bordered with fine lines from smoking cigarettes all his life, but they retained their delicacy. He was dark complected for a white man, and his poorly executed blue line tattoos, most likely drawn in a jailhouse somewhere, were almost undetectable on his rippling forearms. Jimmie was good looking, no one doubted that, like a faded movie star who always played the bad guy. He drove around town in Jude's truck and always seemed to be busy, yet the house and yard looked like a wreck from the road.

"I'm sure he'll appreciate it," Jimmie said as he took the plate.

I didn't let it go. "Can I go see him?"

"Buddy," his voice quaked, "he ain't up for no visitors today." His eyes seemed to be welling up. I released the plate into his hands. "But I'll try to get him ready for you to come back tomorrow. Damn, this smells good. You got my number?" I nodded, even though I didn't.

When the screen door banged shut, I felt like a coward. I should have fought him to see Jude, no matter what state he was in. But if I pressed Jimmie, I thought he might break. I couldn't tell if it was an act.

I drove back home faster, the night falling early, the smell of brush burning. I imagined Jude doped up and moaning in his bed, and Jimmie ravaging the plate of food I had made, not even noticing how pretty it was.

Jude was the picture of health just a few months before. The summer had kissed his arms and face pink. A little wisp of silver hair lay over the top of his head. He always wore the same uniform, even in the heat of the summer: long khaki pants, a white T-shirt, over which he buttoned a short-sleeved, collared shirt all the way to the very top.

On a sweltering day last July, we had scampered over flooded timber, through vines and briars. I could barely keep up, even though I was almost twenty years younger. Jude led me to an old-growth forest that was cool and dark.

It was one of the best days of my life. Just me, Jude, and his plants. He wove together the forest's narratives, evolutionary history, and power. He embraced its beauty without needing anything in return. He revealed this landscape and his imagination to me—a multidimensional floral world, extending all around us, from the topmost leaves to the depths of the water table.

I was an adult when I first met Jude, and I couldn't believe anyone like this was a part of my family. I had heard about a relative who studied science, but we never visited with him when I was a kid. Apparently, he knew about me too. When we were first introduced at my grandmother's funeral he said, "Oh, yes, the artist," beaming. My chosen career was something no one in my family knew how to talk about, except as some kind of disability. Jude always inquired about it. He admired it.

On our walk, we carried a pouch of field corn to bait the traps for the droves of nocturnal wild hogs that rummaged through the woods and dug up the plants he loved. He pointed to the black ground and said, "They're ravenous." But I couldn't tell if the soil was torn up or not.

In the darkest part of the forest, Jude recognized a plant with the glee of a crush. "Well, hello, beautiful," he said, introducing me to an awkward tree crouching near the massive trunk of a poplar. "This is the *Magnolia macrophylla*. The big leaf magnolia." Jude lifted the tip of a huge droopy leaf with his index finger. He peeked underneath and said, "Not one aphid." He offered the tree a congratulatory grin.

He turned to me. "It has the biggest leaves of any tree in North America. It's an understory tree. Extremely fragile."

"How does it survive in this dark?" I asked.

"Not very well at all. They don't produce viable seeds here. They just cling to a space and try to get tall enough to survive." He sounded resigned. "That's why they grow these huge and beautiful leaves." He spread one out to show me. It was the size of a man's torso, with threadlike ribs supporting translucent flesh. Jude let the leaf relax, and then he ran his hands up the tree's skinny trunk, coaxing it to arch down so he could see its fruiting body. He peered inside the apical bud and pinched the base of the top leaf, testing its give. He said something to the tree that I couldn't quite hear, then let the tree lurch back into the posture of a wiry teenager. Jude put his hands on his hips, nodded to himself, and said, "They are very decorative."

We left the tree looking shy and disheveled, but even from a distance, its leaves glowed in the forest.

That was the last walk in the woods I ever took with Jude. I went back to see him in September, but he didn't feel like going anywhere with me. He tried to get comfortable in his chair. I told him about my exhibitions, a subject he was usually curious about, but he seemed distracted. We ran out of things to say to each other. I fidgeted and made his dogs restless. I guess he felt obliged to have one more show-and-tell, and he finally struggled up and took me with him to check on his greenhouse. Jimmie watched us from the porch, a lean silhouette.

Jude's greenhouse was the size of a closet. He made it out of old windows and a storm door—or had it made, by Jimmie, who was lousy at construction. You could barely see the structure for the vines that covered it. They had let it all go.

Jimmie had rigged it up with a yard sprinkler hung upside down from the ceiling attached to a garden hose that ran all the way to the back-porch faucet such that Jude could reach over and turn it on from his chair. Every morning when he drank his coffee and every evening when he ate his dinner, he made it rain.

All spring, the plants had patiently pressed their fronds against the glass until they pried their way outside. The exterior of the greenhouse bloomed in rare vines, while the inside burgeoned with countless species of wildflowers.

"I'm so sorry about this mess. I've got to cut this all back," he said, as if he actually would. "That clematis is going to take over everything." The admonishment in his voice disguised delight.

There was one plant in the greenhouse that he did not chide for growing too fast: the *sulcata* orange tree. It was a tree by name only, just over two feet high and struggling. It looked out of place. Jude had fashioned wire coat hangers and sticks to train the vines to adhere to a guarded perimeter around the tree.

It was a tropical plant that couldn't be watered too much, so Jude had hung a sheet of plastic above the tree like a floating shroud. He checked the texture of its soil. He plucked a desiccated leaf and let it fall. He cupped the tiny orange in his hand to test its weight. It was healthy and dense. And even though the plant looked weak, inside the fruit, a seed set was forming that Jude intended to propagate, but never did.

After Christmas, I heard that Jude had canceled a springtime trip he organized for the Kiwanis Club to go to British Columbia to see the Butchart Gardens. For as long as I knew him, Jude had fantasized about the infinite varieties of roses there. It worried everyone in town that he wasn't going.

I called to wish him happy New Year.

"He's still not feeling well," Jimmie said, answering Jude's phone.

"Let me bring you something," I said.

"We're okay. I need to get him rested. We're going to the doctor tomorrow. It's his back."

"Has he been up walking? That's what he needs. To get outside."

"I'm doing best I can with him."

"I can come out there right now and help you."

"He's asleep right now. Maybe some other time."

Jimmie didn't trust me. I hadn't been inside their home since Jimmie moved in. People around here don't understand their kind of relationship, but I didn't judge them. I understood Jude—a brilliant scientist and a profound historian. A professor. My kindred spirit.

I had an intuition that Jude was hooked on painkillers. He had a hunger in his eyes. I imagined Jimmie was the source, but I couldn't prove it.

I was close to organizing an intervention when I got a call from my dad. The doctors had found cancer in Jude's lower spine, and it had metastasized all over. It had grown into his brain. Stage four. Six weeks.

About six weeks later, I drove to the hospital in Columbia to see Jude for the last time. I stopped by his house on the way. Winter had struck the trees bare. The place was abandoned. Jimmie had been run off by the parishioners soon after Jude was admitted. They found him alone in the driveway, sitting in Jude's truck listening to music. No one knew where he went after that. I climbed the stairs to the porch where Jude and I had last talked. The hose was still hooked up to the faucet, but the greenhouse hadn't been watered in weeks. The vines growing on the outside of the greenhouse had shed all their leaves, which made it much easier to find the door. Inside, it was warm and fecund.

The plants in pots on the shelves had withered, but their seeds had fallen into the seams between the floorboards. They hit soil where no deer or wild hog could venture. They grew, uninhibited by the competition of the outside world.

The orange tree, however, was almost dead. Its once-hearty leaves fell off at the hint of a breath. Its limbs had dried like bones. Jude could probably nurse it back to life, but I was just here for a second, and after I left, there was no one who could turn on the rain. The single orange was shriveled and leathery. I snatched it from its limb and headed to the hospital.

The nurses on the fourth floor wheeled carts across floors polished to reflection. Monitors chirped in the distance. No one was expecting me. I wandered the halls, unsure if they would let me see him. I lingered in the waiting-room area where *Better Homes and Gardens* magazines lay feathered out like a card trick. Solemn parents hunched in chairs while their toddler roamed around their legs. A nurse came in. "Ms. Andrews?" An older woman collected herself and obediently followed. What was I waiting on? My name to be called? I decided to go find Jude myself.

I rounded the corner. A giant white board loomed over the nurses' station.

FAIRE E J, Room 216.

I went for it, 202, then 204. I avoided eye contact with nurses, and my gaze was drawn into the open doors. Bare backs were half-sheathed in fallen blue gowns and tangled in white sheets, like sinking in snow. Faces emerged from the frost, mouths agape. White vines ran into their noses. In 208, a whole back was exposed and an arm draped off the bed rail. The rooms were shady, and there was a smell you could almost see—sharp and glistening on top of every other odor.

Around a corner, the west side of the building swallowed the light, creating shadows of the supply carts in the hallway. Half the nurse's face was aglow. "Can I help you?"

"I'm going to 216," I said, instead of saying his name. "All right," she said, flashing away with an armful of eyedroppers.

The corridor took an angle, and I was facing north. The windows were bathed in blue. I had clear passage down the hallway. I smelled urine.

In 216, Jude was lying on his back facing the window. I came in from behind his headboard. The urine was his, dripping from his sheets, running down a black cable under the bed, puddling on the floor. His hand was on his bald head, and I could see the tips of his yellow toenails.

I rounded the bed, and saw that Jude was completely naked, but not bare. A bougainvillea vine and a mother of chestnut. A clematis and four versions of wild gardenia.

A drape of wood anemone with its five sepals blossomed around the dorsum of his foot, winding up his ankle. His right calf was covered in golden aster; his left was a swath of creeping phlox, the lavender variety, a sea of purple pink petals dotted by golden anthers. They gave way to a bouquet of jewelweed in bloom, yellow funnel blossoms, with the spur drawn in a perfect teardrop. Two fringed polygalas, one red, one purple, entwined his scrotum, their flaring sepals disappeared underneath. His penis was a coralroot orchid. The sepal fanned across his groin and the anther cap was the tip. His waist was wrapped in *Wisteria frutescens*. The sinewy vines seemed to constrict him, but bursting through the rugged wood was purple chicory blossom, a ragged sailor, its pistil filigreed white and its style red inside Jude's flat navel. The forest went from Appalachian to coastal on his upper body. On his right breast was drawn the jarring apex of a longleaf pine frond, the needles painted in three colors: iridescent emerald, night-forest green, and a strip of rich ocher. A purple pollen cone was erect across his right nipple, so real it was sticky looking. His left nipple was the apex of a leaf of the *Magnolia macrophylla*, life-sized. Pale greens, shaded veins, and a prominent midrib engulfed Jude's entire rib cage, done in a translucent jade. The base of the leaf and its petiole wrapped around his back unseen. His sternum was a bed of dayflowers, Solomon's seal, and Queen Anne's lace that were pruned sharp at his collar line, where he always buttoned up his shirt, where his skin was just skin.

I couldn't even say hello. I just stood there breathing. My shadow breached his face, and he stirred, "Oh, hello. I'm such a mess. I am so sorry about this mess. I am so glad you are here. I'm going to clean up. Please. I'm such a mess. I'm so sorry. I'm very ill and made such a mess."

I have friends with elaborate tattoos, but I had never seen such color and dimension. Jude's skin had become so pale and white, almost translucent, and the artist's ink seemed to be filled with light coming from within. Before I could say anything, the nurse came in. "Oh my, I didn't know he would have

visitors. I just left for a second. I didn't know he was like this. Let me get him cleaned up so you two can visit."

There was an awkward silence. What was left of his consciousness was pure politesse. "Yes. Yes, ma'am. Thank you. I'm just fine. This is my friend."

The nurse got between Jude and me and motioned me out the door. "Just wait outside, sir, and come back in a few minutes. I'll have him all ready for you."

I walked around in the corridor and stole glances of the faces sinking into the snow. After Jude's body, the rooms seemed whiter. My eyes had acclimated briefly to the color of the tropics, or springtime in the mountains. I stared into a room where a woman was turned away, running her fingers through her hair. Her gown was open and I could see her back, brown with dark spots, the notches of her spine, her flexible, sheathed skeleton displaying the elaborate mechanics of breathing.

No one had ever mentioned Jude's tattoos. I assume no one in the community had ever seen his body. What did it feel like to know your body was both a dangerous secret and a beautiful revelation? In a place where fantasies for young boys are molded into shooting a ten-point buck or catching the winning pass, how did Jude find his? Was wearing this skin a labor of love? Was his body in a constant state of release under his clothes? Was this evidence of a double life or just a single one, folded like a private note and kept inside the envelope? Who received this gift? Was it Jimmie?

I wanted to know everything. Surely, he could trust me.

I am an artist.

But those blooms were not for my eyes.

The nurse found me in the hallway. "He's ready for you now," she said.

I went back in. Jude and his bed were crisply cleaned, and his gown was tied neatly around his back. The jungle forest had disappeared. His forearms were bare white. Still, his shoulder around the edges of the gown and his shin that showed through the folds of the blanket were evidence of a planet in bloom.

I gather he was embarrassed for me to see the jungle he had meticulously hidden for so long, so I avoided mentioning it. "I picked the orange from your tree," I said. It was the size of a handball. "Would you like a slice?"

"Yes. The orange, the Sanbokan orange. *Sulcata*. Yes. No. You take it. I'm not hungry. It's still growing in the greenhouse? *Sulcata*. Yes, I would like to taste it. Yes. Yes. So sweet. Impossible to grow here. Native to the equator. But grown in Japan. A colleague brought me a wild seed from Malaysia. Still growing. *Citrus sulcata*."

I finally got the courage to say, "I love your ink."

"Yes. Oh, that. Well. I don't . . . Why, thank you, Jeff. I go to an upstanding gentleman in Charlotte. Very well-respected. An artist of his trade."

I was nervous about the orange. I sliced it open, and its juice was darker than its skin. It flowed out down the blade of the knife, down my arm, and dripped off my elbow to stain the sheet.

"Wow, that's a juicy orange," I told Jude, to his delight.

"Yes, they survive long periods of drought. Tropical coasts."

I put a slice into his hand. His palm had lost its pink, was white, like the sheets. The juice from the orange pooled up in a yellow puddle in his hand and left a yellow stain trailing down his chin and neck.

"They'll have to clean you up again," I joked.

"Yes. Yes, they will. Hmm. Sweet acidic." He managed to hold a seed in his fingers and squeezed it, testing its give. He held it close to his eyes and examined the seed's shape and texture. He said yes to himself, and rolled over on his side away from me and fell asleep.

His resplendent back gleamed through the parting of the gown. An orange flowering vine that began in the crack of his ass disappeared, winding around his waist. I was embarrassed, but I stared, until I heard footsteps in the hall. I covered him up with the cotton blanket, then left.

The next time I saw Jude was at his funeral. The members of the church were there, the Kiwanis Club, and a few botanists who taught at nearby colleges. They told stories about intrepid hikes into uncharted swamplands behind Dollar General stores and finding the rare *Helonias bullata*. One told of how he and Jude had found a species new to science in a patch of oconee bells on the side of the road in Georgia. Inside the casket were bouquets of weeds, each with tiny inch-wide flowers of a variety of shapes and colors. Each bouquet was different, and each was made by a botanist. His collar was buttoned to his neck, of course, and he wore an awkward tie. Onto his hands, crossed at his chest, someone had sprinkled tiny maroon seeds. Dust to dust, man of mud.

The serviceberry has bloomed.
The casket was sealed and lowered.
Buried my kindred alive.

Jeff Whetstone is a professor of photography and the director of the program for visual arts at Princeton University.

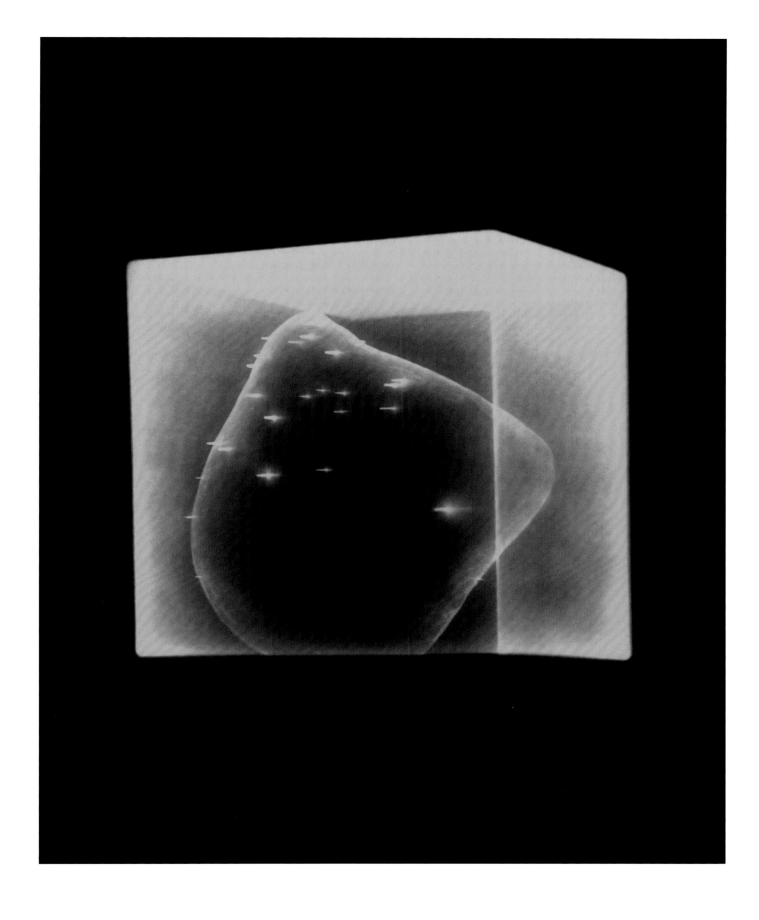

MAO TSE TUNG

ARRHYTHMIC MYTHIC RA

# creative capitalism[1]
## The Visual Artists' News Sheet |
## March-April 2011

"We have to live this dead reality, this mad transition, in the same way that we lived prison, as a strange and ferocious way of reaffirming life. You could not escape the atrocious experience of prison, the contact with death and its violence. [...] We were constrained to suffer dark romantic hallucinations. There was no longer any alternative. Certainly for us, there has never been any alternative to the world, but always an alternative in the world. A la Rauschenberg: a world that is assumed, shattered, reinvented in the form of its monstrosity. But even the possibility of such a heroism was denied to us. [...] We have to live and suffer the defeat of truth, of our truth. We have to destroy its representation, its continuity, its memory, its trace. All subterfuges for avoiding the recognition that reality has changed, and with it truth, have to be rejected. [...] The very blood in our veins had been replaced."
— Antonio Negri, *Art and Multitude*[2]

Negri's *Art and Multitude* consists of nine letters, most of which were written to his friends at the end of the 1980s while he was in exile in France. Negri here describes the destitution that the left endured after the defeats of the 1970s: the destruction of all its hopes, the way in which it had been outflanked by a neoliberalism which successfully installed business thinking into all areas of everyday life. What emerges here, in other words, is an account of the immediate after-effects of the installation of what I have called capitalist realism: the view that, since there is no alternative to capitalism, the only possible attitude consists in adjusting to its demands. Negri poses the left's predicament very acutely.

To go back to the seeming certainties of older forms of militancy would be to consign oneself to irrelevance, obsolescence, to become an historical relic; but to accept the new situation, to adapt to it, would be to concede total defeat. The only possibility, Negri suggests, is to endure the time in the desert as a kind of religious trial: a moment of terrible and terrifying

431

renewal, a transformation of the revolutionary subject happening at the very moment when revolution seems impossible and the forces of reaction control everything. The new situation — capital's mutation into a post-Fordist form in which labour becomes "immaterial", "flexible" and subject to the pressures of globalisation — offers new potentials, which must be embraced.

Reading these at times extraordinary communications, I find myself, as ever, persuaded by Negri's negative analysis, his vision of culture and consciousness totally subsumed by capital. What I am much less convinced by is his positive alternative to this banal yet dark dominion. Like his inspirations, Deleuze and Guattari, Negri is a vitalist who opposes capital's necrotic force to the living potenza of the creativity of the multitude.

Art, Negri maintains, is intrinsically rebellious and subversive. Even though Negri himself recognises the dangers of taking too much consolation in art, he ends up retaining faith in it. "When I myself suffered the political defeat of the seventies and in the depths of despair, asked art to help me to endure it and to help me find individual ways of resistance and redemption", Negri writes, "I was overestimating the capacity of art." Yet Negri is soon arguing that art is a "perennial demonstration of the irreducibility of freedom, of subversive action, of love for radical transformation".

From Negri's point of view, there is no contradiction between these two claims. What he is arguing is that an individual can never find his way out of despondency through art alone; rather, it is only by new forms of solidarity — which necessarily must involve art — that escape is possible. While the point about collectivity has never been more pressing, Negri's hymning of art seems strangely nostalgic. For the era of capitalist realism has also seen all kinds of synergies between art and business, nowhere better summed up than in the concept of the "creative industries".

It is of course possible to argue that the art that has dominated in capitalist realism, its artistic and commercial value massively inflated, is a fake art, a betrayal and dilution of art's inherent militancy. But why not go all the way with Negri's logic of negativity, and argue that there is no readymade, already-existing utopian energy; that there is nothing which, by its very nature, resists incorporation into capital? So it is not then a matter of creativity versus capitalism — or rather of capitalism as the capturing of the creativity of the multitude. Instead, the enemy now could better be called creative capitalism, and overcoming it will not involve inventing new modes of positivism, but new kinds of negativity.

ARRHYTHMIC MYTHIC RA

Simone White

let fani willis fuck

i recently clocked in
to interview a very famous person
at not even half the worth of my time given
the need to corral precursively
a completely wild feeling inside my head
over and over he would insert "just"
before the predicate noun he chose to describe
what were in fact indescribable
riddles
irreducible forms of trouble
violent confrontations between the inside and outside of a
        given living host
what he has done
is eliminate a reductive grammar from the realm of pictures
it is his achievement; it is not emotional not like what i do
generative of envy
the technological glamour of his work; its digital appendages
awareness of envy "just"
printing
for example
the edit suite
that has to be consulted along with
several of the world's great technicians of pictures in order
        to isolate
what he sees
as possibility
to learn that the machines cannot make it possible then "just"
returning to performers who breathe hair straightening or
        white silk blouses
mannered yet penis-bound
femininity
this floral threat
he understands surely
is against minimalism or reduction as a poetic principle it
        is excess
even excessive
hey, look, it's only genius it's only
say no one else can steal the way i steal it's nigger sleight
        of hand
the curator thinks
it's historical we'll let him have it
i think
i'm sick of hearing about
that man's international power the way his name arrives
in conversation
a fire blanket unfurls between roman columns
i am petty like that
this thing i am paid to preview is so beautiful
it causes wincing and cowering in my attention
let me say i hesitate to approach the broken or what i called
        wild state of the plaintiff this thing found
i will often resort to the eggshell skull rule as a rhetorical tic
        but it is a jewel of the common law and so
to be honest
i am not sure which sin i am invoking
whether it is envy actually
or uncut desire

if i cannot have communion with another human
lord give me the elements of withstanding to witness your
        creatures'
darkness
i wince and duck from the unkempt harm of having been
        betrayed
just
one
too many times
my person hates my love which threatens the exchange value
        of love
i think my love is out of capital and therefore nothing no one
        can tolerate it and so when confronted with this fable
of blackness lifted out of the universe
pure black
as an incursion upon the sexual phantasm of the black pimp
the black
rips the scabs off
the wild feeling the death grief
scattering random burnholes around
what is realistic
the way i wake up to chase's rude warnings regarding my
        insolvency
and the nightmare white woman who has been offered
        freedom to assault me keeps shrieking whore
what am i supposed to do
god. i am such whore? readymade perfect toilet
this scenario wherein the child whore is redeemed
by a moralistic psychopath
is this it
i do want to be taken
by a black wave made of something there is no name for

**Simone White is a poet and associate professor of English at the University of Pennsylvania.**

off
off
off
off

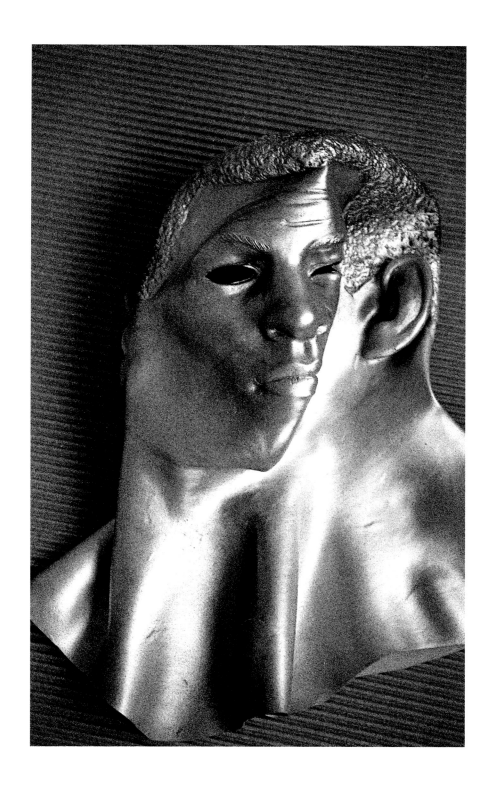

ARRHYTHMIC MYTHIC RA

ARRHYTHMIC MYTHIC RA

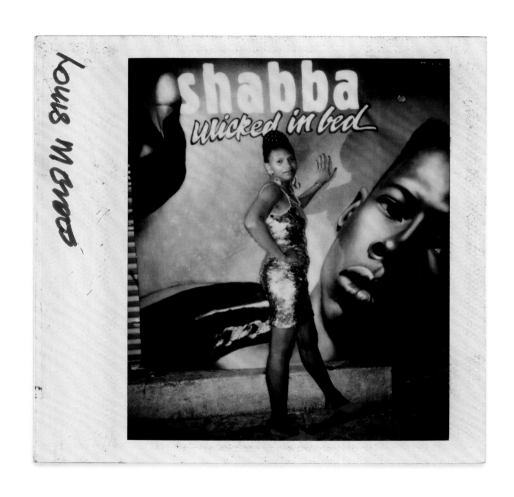

Ben Okri

Impossible Truths

These pictures, each one, turn on
Something mysteriously gruesome.
What it is one can't say, except
That they are real and that nothing
Unnatural constitutes the amazement
They bring to the domestic gaze.
Reality here is uneasy, not because
Anything unusual is happening,
But because what you see puzzles the
Grasp. When reality exceeds itself
There's often a school of art to give
It a name, make it familiar to the mind.
But these images resist the familiar,
Because nothing unusual persists about them.
Only a picture of a dead woman on a wall
Upside down, beneath which sits an eternally
Grieving daughter, strong in grief and in gaze.
Then there's the child with a mask that has no
Features, a gold featureless face in a land
That long ago was poisoned by the love of gold
From the west. Then there's the wedding
Couple covered in paper money stapled or glued
To their clothes. They look at us from the dim
Side of prosperity, poverty's shadow. A mood
Of hovels lingers in the bright colors. A woman,
Naked and pregnant, reclines on a naked stair.
Her gaze is defiant, and on her feet is a tag
That tells us that her freedom has its limits
And yet what tag or bars could cage the tigress
In her soul. In another picture, an ancient
African god appears, but unseen, syncretic, brought
Thousands of miles across an enslaved
Sea. The camera's eye turns inward
Faced with these subjects. It refuses to record.
Instead it caresses impossible truths, making
The eye take on some of the throb of the heart.
To see here is to feel something that language
Is poor to express, lives we'll never see, a
Way we would never know how to be. The
Courage of life here shakes the boundaries
Around which we live. And a child here shows
More resilience than many a soldier in a grim war.
To survive the wars that power wreaks on these
Children who eat injustice with the grain
Of each breakfast, to smile when a century
Of history has worn away the edges of the soul,
And to still have the grip on life in the falling
Light, gives a new tinge to the heroic.
Sometimes a photograph shows us more than
An unseen cage. A single image stuns the silence.

Ben Okri is a Nigerian British poet, essayist, and novelist.

ISBN 3-928762-42-7

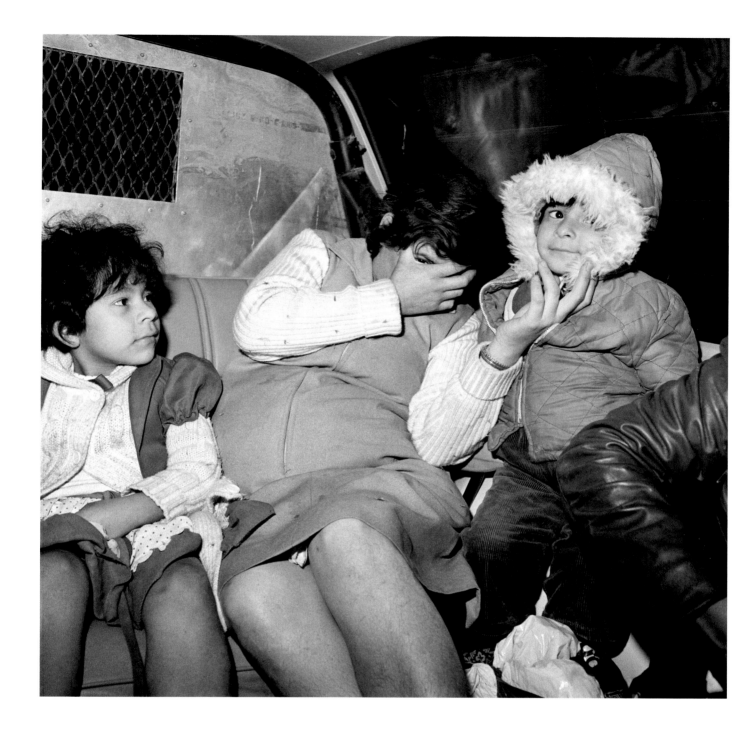

ARRHYTHMIC MYTHIC RA

ARRHYTHMIC MYTHIC RA

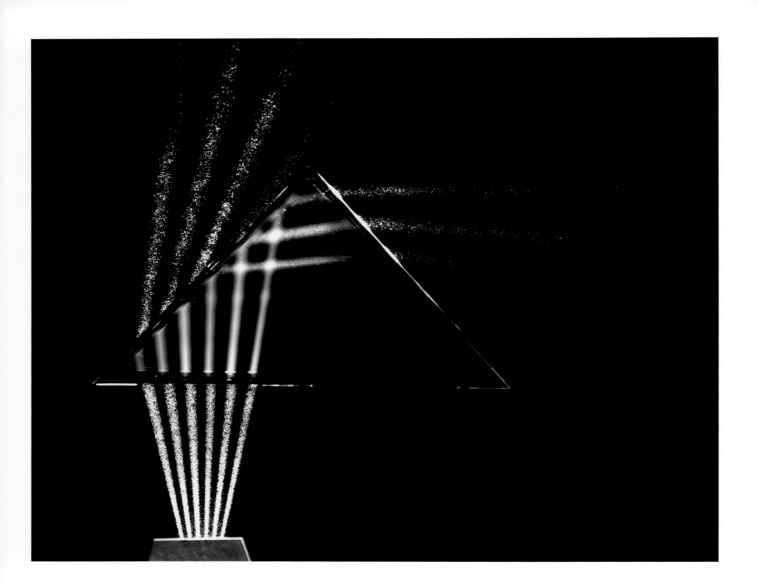

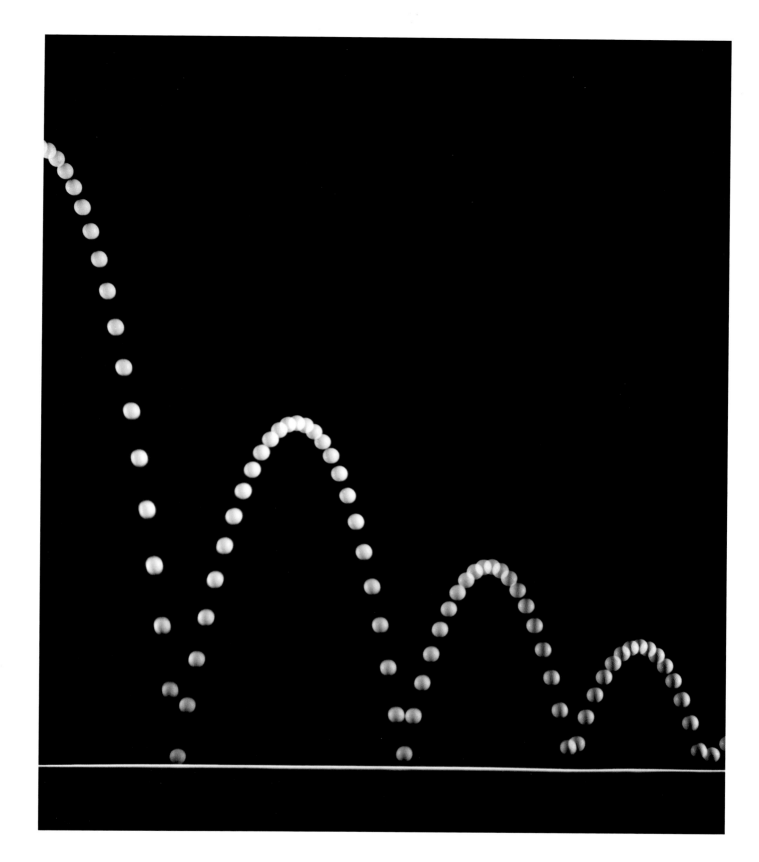

ARRHYTHMIC MYTHIC RA

ARRHYTHMIC MYTHIC RA

Jason Hickel

Imagination

We live in a shadow of the society we could have.

It seems strange to say such a thing, as we are repeatedly informed that we live in the best of all possible worlds, aside, perhaps, from a few rough bits around the edges. But anyone who pays any attention at all can see immediately that this is not true. The reality of ecological crisis stares every sane observer in the face, with accelerating climate breakdown and mass destruction of species. And we confront an obvious social crisis, too, with billions of people unable to meet even their most basic needs, such as nutritious food and clean water.

These are not difficult problems to solve. Maintaining a stable biosphere? Ensuring people have access to essential goods? These are *basics*, and easy to achieve. They should be the first principles of any sane civilization. Yet in our existing system, they appear totally intractable, nearly impossible to achieve. In fact, we are openly encouraged to resign ourselves to misery. "There is no alternative," Margaret Thatcher told us. You must accept the reality that has been decreed, and if you dare to try anything else, we will crush you.

How strange, for a culture that claims to value freedom. For a people who say they celebrate independence and creativity. And yet, we swallowed their words and repeated them to one another: "There is no alternative."

What accounts for our inability to deal swiftly with the crises we face? The answer is quite straightforward. It is because most of us have little, if any, control over the direction of our society. We do not have democracy in any meaningful sense at all. Yes, of course, some of us live in democratic *political* systems, where we get to elect political figures from time to time. But when it comes to the *economic* system—the system of production—not even the shallowest illusion of democracy is allowed to enter.

There is a fairy tale we have been told: that capitalism is just a system of businesses and markets and trade. It's just people producing and selling things to one another, and what could possibly be wrong with that? But the story is wrong. Businesses and markets and trade existed for thousands of years before capitalism. Capitalism is a relatively recent system, only about five hundred years old. If one was to point to the single most important trait that defines this particular economic system, it would be that it is fundamentally antidemocratic.

Under capitalism, our enormous productive capacities are controlled by *capital*: the major financial firms, the large corporations, and the one percent who own the majority of investable assets. Capital determines what gets produced, how our labor and resources are used and for whose benefit. And for capital, the *purpose* of production is not to meet people's needs, or to achieve progress on social and ecological goals. The purpose is to maximize and accumulate profit—that is the overriding objective. Capital, therefore, shapes the material world around us, and we are all held hostage to its wishes.

As a result, we get wildly perverse forms of production. Our labor and resources are mobilized to churn out things such as fossil fuels, SUVs, fast fashion, mansions, cruise ships, private jets, industrial beef, aircraft carriers, advertising, and tear gas. Totally unnecessary things that mostly serve the interests of capital accumulation and elite consumption. Why? Because these things are profitable to capital. Meanwhile, we suffer chronic shortages of urgently needed things such as renewable energy, public transit, affordable housing, and so on. It should, therefore, come as no surprise that despite extremely high levels of aggregate output—and high levels of energy and material use that are driving ecological breakdown—deprivation remains widespread in the capitalist world economy.

Capitalism also limits our technology. This is strange for people to hear because we are so often told the opposite, that capitalism is all about innovation. But it's not. Capital doesn't innovate. *People* innovate. Capital simply directs our innovative capacity to what is most profitable to capital. So, we get huge investment in the innovation of things such as advertising algorithms and military drones and fracking technologies but massive underinvestment in the innovation of lifesaving medicines or integrated public transit or longer-lasting, upgradable, and repairable smartphones.

It doesn't have to be this way. Over the past few years, scientists have demonstrated that we can provision good lives for all eight billion people on this planet—including nutritious diets, modern housing, heating, cooling, clean water, clean energy, universal health care, education, public transit, refrigerators, induction stoves, and laptops—with around 70 percent less energy and material extraction than the global economy presently uses, which would enable us to decarbonize fast enough to limit global warming to 1.5 degrees Celsius and also reverse biodiversity loss. This is incredibly good news. It represents what *could* be achieved if we had democratic control over production. We could eliminate poverty and ensure well-being for all while also arresting ecological breakdown. And we could do it *fast*.

We know this from empirical evidence. Using both social experiments and real-world studies, scientists have found that when people have direct democratic control over resources, they overwhelmingly prioritize social and ecological goals. We also know this from the official citizens' assemblies that have been convened in France, Spain, and Great Britain, where people have demonstrated that they are able to reach consensus with astonishing speed: scale down destructive and unnecessary forms of production; focus on what is necessary for well-being and ecology. People *already know* what needs to be done.

Some say they find it difficult to imagine a postcapitalist society. It seems so ethereal, so out of reach. This glitch in our mental capacities is remarkable given that for 99.7 percent of our two-hundred-thousand-year history, we have organized production and exchange in a wide variety of noncapitalist ways. The historical record is packed with examples of noncapitalist societies, including highly complex urban civilizations with cosmopolitan cultures, advanced innovations, and long-distance trade. In the arc of human history, capitalism—a monopoly of elites over the means of production—has been an aberration, and a brief one at that, imposed violently through enclosures and colonization in the face of fierce resistance. Even during the twentieth century, most popular movements—from the labor movements in Europe to the anticolonial movements across the Global South—believed that human progress would ultimately require overcoming the tyranny of capital. This stuff is in our bones.

What would a postcapitalist society look like today? There are basically two pillars. The first is universal public services. If you can imagine a society where the core essentials of life—housing, health care, education, transit, water, energy, et cetera—are decommodified and produced in a way that ensures sufficient access for all, you are halfway there. The second is economic democracy. If you can imagine democracy in the workplace, including in private firms—where we, the workers, collectively decide what to produce, how to use resources, and how to distribute our surplus, and where the primary objective of production is to improve society rather than to maximize profit—that's the rest of it. That's a postcapitalist economy.

What's interesting is that both of these principles are wildly popular. In poll after poll, survey after survey, they enjoy striking majority support. We *already* want such a world. We can already *imagine* it. We all know in our hearts what a better world would be. This is why that mantra—"there is no alternative"—needed to be repeated so forcefully. Not because an alternative is in fact out of reach but, rather, because it is always so near at hand.

Jason Hickel is an economic anthropologist, author, and a fellow of the Royal Society of Arts.

ARRHYTHMIC MYTHIC RA

*Back view*

Close up view

ARRHYTHMIC MYTHIC RA

ARRHYTHMIC MYTHIC RA

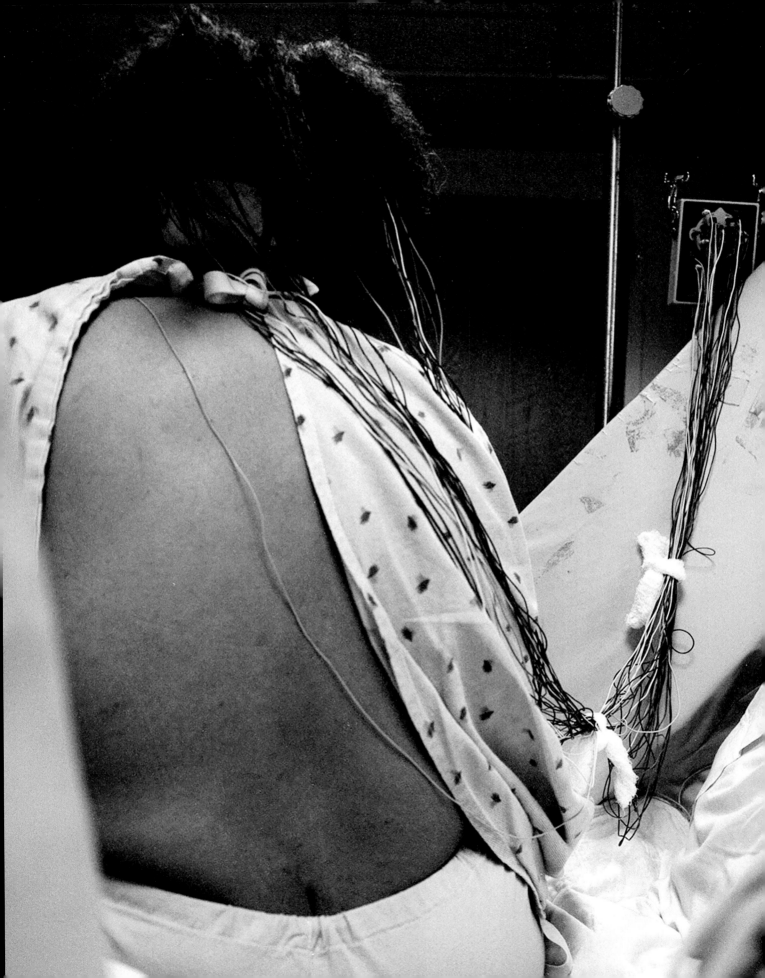

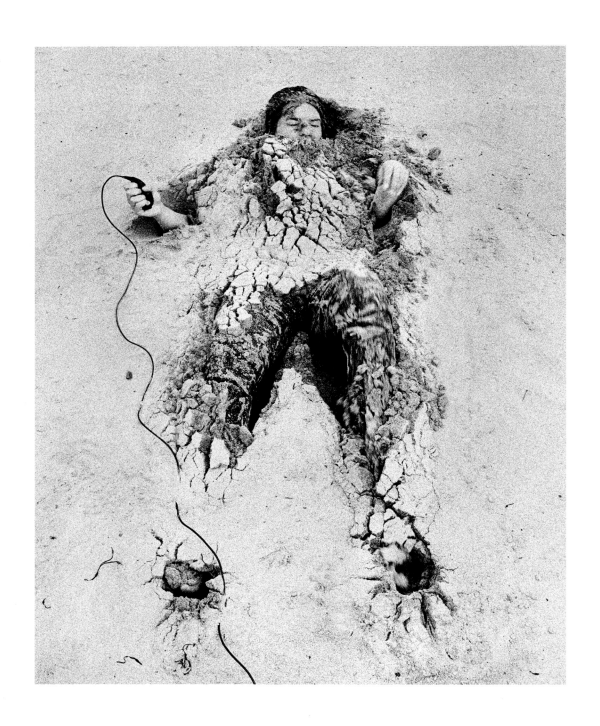

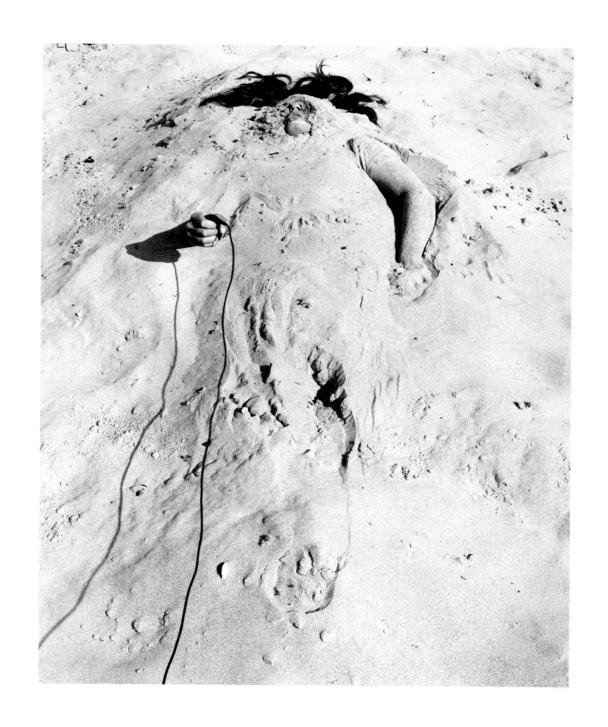

ARRHYTHMIC MYTHIC RA

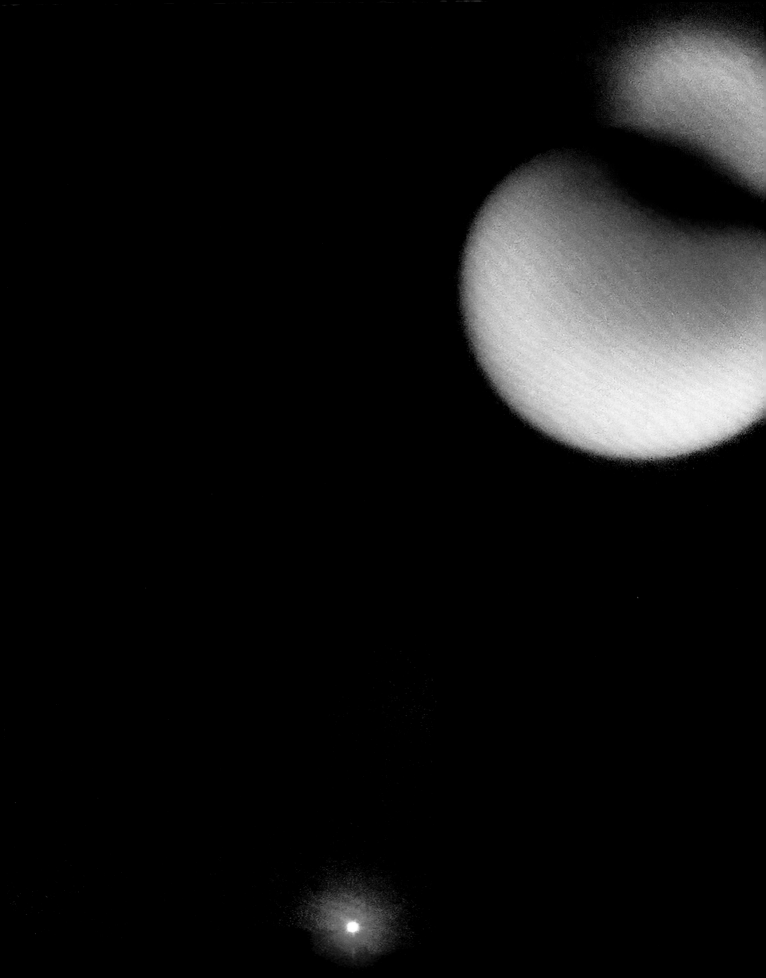

Tracy K. Smith

'Tis of Thee

Born into a greedy land, but not to feed it.
*Play with fire, but you best not feed it.*

The appetite for truth is cavernous. Too
Many brought here. Bought. Not to feed it.

What you whispered up close, tooth to ear.
Trust flew. Very few thought not to feed it.

Drive you to a picnic near a big black tree.
Rope-snap. Flame-crack. Plot not to feed it.

Ushered freedom into a big drafty house.
Stood there, hands bare. Got naught to feed it.

**Tracy K. Smith is a poet, memoirist, and translator.**

ARRHYTHMIC MYTHIC RA

**Photographs and works:**

**Pages 42-43:**
Adam Broomberg and Oliver Chanarin, *Rene Vallejo Psychiatric Hospital, Cuba,* 2013
Courtesy the late estate of Broomberg and Chanarin

**Pages 44-49:**
Lieko Shiga, *Satounara, Sayounara,* from *Rasen Kaigan,* 2010; *Time Capsules,* from *Rasan Kaigan,* 2010; *Onagawa Tunnel,* 2024
Courtesy the artist

**Pages 50, 56, and 57:**
Balarama Heller, *Zero at the Bone,* 2017; *Angel,* 2023; *Angel 2,* 2023
Courtesy the artist

**Page 55:**
Jeff Whetstone, *John E. Crossing Betty Branch,* 2014
Courtesy the artist

**Pages 58-59:**
Stefan Ruiz, *Samuel "SAMMY" Martinez, Monterrey, Mexico,* 2011; *Michel, Monterrey, Mexico,* 2011
Courtesy the artist

**Pages 60-61:**
Weegee, *Lady Greyhound, the Pompous Pooch,* ca. 1964; *Mao Tse Tung,* ca. 1966
© the artist/International Center of Photography/ Getty Images

**Pages 62-63:**
Sally Mann, *Georgia, Untitled (Cracked Field),* 1996; pages 64-65: *Battlefields, Cold Harbor (Battle),* 2003
© the artist, courtesy Gagosian Gallery

**Pages 66-67:**
Birney Imes, *The Social Inn, Gunnison,* 1989; *Monkey's Place, Merigold,* 1989
© the artist, courtesy Jackson Fine Art

**Pages 68-69:**
Spread of Mark Fisher's "Creative Capitalism," 2011
From *K-Punk: The Collected and Unpublished Writings* (London: Repeater, 2018)

**Pages 70-71:**
Deana Lawson, *Ivanpah Single Tower,* 2023; *Kareem,* 2023
Courtesy David Kordansky Gallery and Gagosian Gallery

**Page 72:**
Lucy Raven, *Untitled,* 2021
Courtesy Lisson Gallery

**Pages 74-75:**
Liz Johnson Artur, *Paris Ball,* 2021; *A Trap for Judges,* 2022
Courtesy the artist

**Pages 76-77:**
Seiichi Furuya, *Graz 1978,* 1978; *Graz 1981,* 1981
Courtesy the artist

**Pages 78-79:**
Louis Mendes, *Wicked,* 1993; *Someone Special,* 1993
Courtesy the artist

**Page 81:**
Back cover of Allan Sekula's *Fish Story* (Rotterdam: Witte de With; Düsseldorf: Richter Verlag, 1995)

**Pages 82-83:**
Ken Light, *San Ysidro, California,* 1985; *El Paso, Texas,* 1985
© the artist and courtesy Midnight LaFrontera, TBW Books, and Contact Press Images

**Pages 84-85:**
Allan Sekula, *Unsuccessful fishing for sardines off the Portuguese coast, Vigo, Galicia, Spain,* May 1992, from *Fish Story,* 1989-95; *The rechristened* Exxon Valdez *awaiting sea trials after repairs. National Steel and Shipbuilding Company. San Diego harbor,* from *Fish Story,* 1989-95
Courtesy the Allan Sekula Studio

**Pages 86-87:**
Arthur Jafa, *Foxy Lady,* 2021; *Wooten,* 2021
Courtesy the artist

**Pages 88-89:**
Berenice Abbott, *Light Through a Prism,* 1958-61; *Bouncing Ball Time Exposure,* 1958-61
Getty Images

**Pages 90-91:**
Trevor Paglen, *Singleton/ SBWASS-R1 and Three Unidentified Space-craft (Space Based Wide Area Surveillance System; USA 32),* 2012; *CLOUD #865 Hough Circle Transform,* 2019
© the artist and courtesy Altman Siegel, San Francisco, and Pace Gallery

**Pages 94-95:**
Kikuji Kawada, *Jumbo Jet,* 1978; *Artificial Moon Trail,* 1969
Courtesy Photo Gallery International, Tokyo

**Pages 96-97:**
Boris Mikhailov, *Untitled,* from *Case History* (1997)
Courtesy the artist

**Pages 98-99:**
Bruce Davidson, *Subway, New York,* 1980,
© the artist/Magnum Photos

**Page 100-101:**
Miroslav Tichý, *Untitled,* ca. 1960-80
Courtesy Tichý Ocean Foundation;
*Untitled,* ca. 1960-80
Courtesy International Center of Photography and Tichý Ocean Foundation

**Pages 102-3:**
Nikki Nelms, *Done Up,* 1994; *Hair Did,* 1995
Courtesy the artist

**Pages 104-5:**
Philip-Lorca diCorcia, *Head #23,* 2001
© the artist and courtesy David Zwirner

**Pages 106-7:**
Paul Kooiker, *Sunday,* 2011
Courtesy the artist

**Pages 108-9:**
Les Krims, *Spectrum Nude,* 1974; *Chicken Pitcher, Pisher, Picture,* 1974
Courtesy the artist

**Pages 110-11:**
Elaine Stocki, *William,* 2008; *Palomino,* 2008
Courtesy the artist and Night Gallery

**Pages 112-13:**
Paul Graham, *Baby and Interview Cubicles, Brixton DHSS, South London,* 1984; *Waiting Area, Hackney DHSS, East London,* 1985
© the artist and courtesy Pace Gallery

**Pages 114-15:**
LaToya Ruby Frazier, *Landscape of the Body (Epilepsy Test),* 2011
Courtesy the artist and Gladstone Gallery

**Pages 116-17:**
Jennifer Calivas, *Self-Portrait While Buried, #7,* 2019; *Self-Portrait While Buried #1,* 2019
Courtesy the artist

**Pages 118-19:**
Harold Eugene Edgerton, *Bullet Through Bulb,* 1936; *Milk Drop Coronet,* 1957
© Harold Edgerton Archive, MIT

**Pages 120-21:**
Kikuji Kawada, *On the Overlapping Moons,* 2021
Courtesy Photo Gallery International, Tokyo

**Page 123:**
Lucy Raven, *Untitled,* 2021
Courtesy Lisson Gallery

Jennifer Calivas, *Self-Portrait While Buried #16*, 2021

# Poetic Record

Photography in a
Transformed World

October 10—11, 2024
Princeton University

A two-day symposium and
concurrent photographic
exhibition at the Hurley Gallery,
Lewis Center for the Arts.

Organized by Deana Lawson, in
collaboration with Jeff Whetstone
and James Welling

For more information, visit:
arts.princeton.edu/poetic-record

LEWIS CENTER PRINCETON | arts

# The Must-Have Classic

## Available once again as an Aperture edition

# The PhotoBook Review

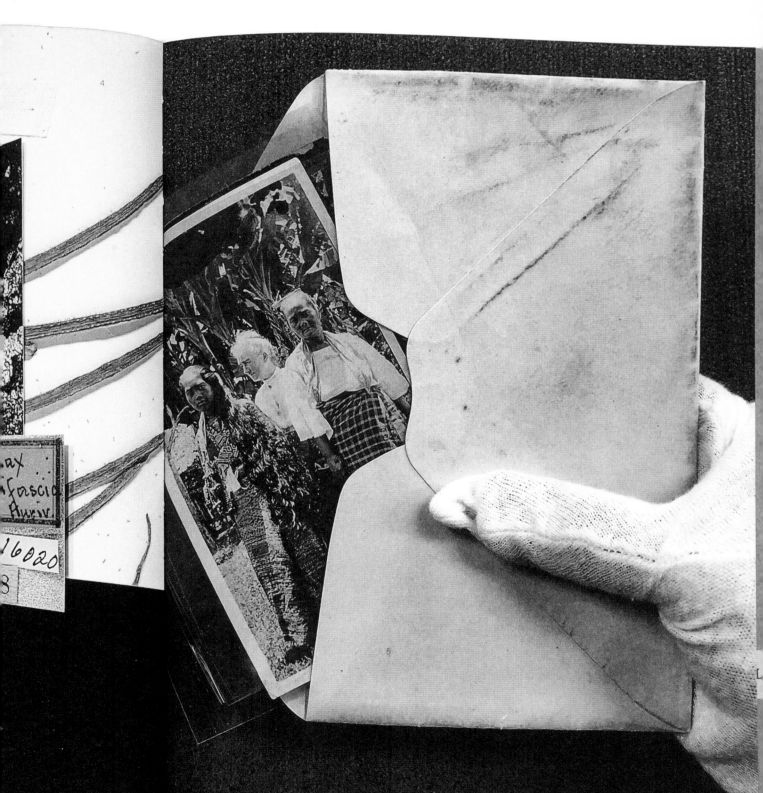

# Unbound Journeys

**Dalia Al-Dujaili in Conversation with Roï Saade**

In 2022, the Beirut-born photographer and designer Roï Saade founded Bound Narratives, a roving archive, workshop, and exhibition program conceived to promote photobooks by Middle Eastern and North African artists. Packing his library into several suitcases, Saade has brought Bound Narratives to Beirut, Florence, Montreal, and Sarajevo, and plans to soon take it to Tunis and Egypt. Here, he discusses the struggle against Eurocentric publishing norms, his process-driven approach, and how photobooks can redraw lines of belonging.

Dalia Al-Dujaili: **Tell me about your journey into bookmaking, curation, and design.**

**Roï Saade**: After a few years in the corporate world, I felt the need to get out of it and work toward something more creatively fulfilling. While studying graphic design at USEK University, in Lebanon, I had taken some photography courses. I found that photography was a means to access communities that I don't belong to, to break these religious and social barriers and just explore Beirut.

And photobooks allowed me to work at the intersection of design and photography. As an editor, I want to recognize work that is not being acknowledged by the industry's gatekeepers, and to counter stereotypical depictions of West Asia and the Arab world. My practice is very research-driven and relies on close collaboration with other artists. I'm attracted to the process rather than the end result.

DA: **Can you tell me about the motivations behind Bound Narratives?**

**RS**: Bound Narratives is a growing archive of photobooks from and about the MENA [Middle East and North Africa] region. It strives to build a broad and open repository of visual materials to stimulate education and critical discourse through photography and digital narrative. In doing so, the archive seeks to remedy an imbalance of cultural knowledge between the Global South and North. The MENA region is very familiar with the American and Eurocentric canon of photography. Our bookstores, libraries, and homes are filled with Western photobooks. Yet it's rare to find photobooks from the region itself in these collections. It was first an internal critique.

We have no shortage of artists or storytellers. In fact, it's the opposite. We have an overwhelming amount. It is the economic and political realities—and the lack of resources and publishers—that disconnect us from each other and from the world. We depend heavily on the West to acknowledge us first and publish our work. And that's why my initiative is to try to create exposure, however minimal it is. Whatever the problems are, try to solve some of them yourself. So, I started a public inventory and started asking my network of artists to share photobooks by artists in the region.

This page:
Cover of Tamara Abdul
Hadi's *Picture an Arab
Man* (We Are the Medium,
2022); opposite: Bound
Narratives at Takeover,
an artist-led project space
in Beirut, April 2023

DA: **I'm wondering what the challenges are. I know you live and work in Canada, but you also do work in Lebanon and in the region as well.**

**RS**: Yeah, I work and live between Lebanon and Canada. The challenges are economic, no doubt. We can't underestimate how the lack of resources and money control what is being seen and how it's being seen. Most of the artists I collaborated with are self-published. Everyone is struggling, fighting for crumbs from Western institutions. And so, you have to try to be creative. You're very limited, and in these limitations, you have to dance and find ways. By contrast, when foreigners parachute to our region to work, they get easily published by someone in the

West. It's very interesting to see that struggle for locals to amplify their voices while foreigners are easily published. At the same time, you can also see a pattern where most of the published artists from the region get to be published in the West by either immigrating, or by living for a period of time or creating these networks in, let's say, France or New York. When it's not foreigners, it's mostly diasporic artists who get wider visibility.

I'm interested in showing these books to local Middle Eastern and North African communities—for them to see what has been produced and what are these cultures around them that are so disconnected and so disrupted by regional politics. I also want to share them with the Global North to say: These narratives exist. There's more than one modernity and contemporary. There are so many worlds in one world, and they can all fit together.

DA: **I love that, many worlds in one world.**

RS: With Bound Narratives, I focus on the book's journey after its production. It's a correspondence of the past and the present. It's an exchange between the artist and the viewer. People sit on the carpets and focus on the book and consume it as a ritual. At Bound Narratives, you don't have to buy a book. You can come to this gathering and look at the

## There are so many worlds in one world, and they can all fit together.

books and experience these books without the need of a financial transaction. What's important is people being together, studying, playing together.

DA: **In 2022, you designed Tamara Abdul Hadi's *Picture an Arab Man*.**

RS: Tamara's book is an attempt to reframe the visual representation of contemporary Arab men. The design choices were informed by how she sees her father, how she sees her cousin, her nephew. So much of the effort was put into small, subtle details—the texture of the cover, the weight of the paper, the bouncing of reflective colors, the empty pages, the repetition of cropped images. I love this cover. It's like burgundy wine. Her father is included. He was an amateur photographer, and she's very inspired by him. The linen texture—how the image almost fades inside it—contributes to an ambiguity we were trying to communicate, as well as the softness and beauty that is very absent in mass-media representations of Arab men.

DA: **That year, you also designed *Dry*, the second photobook by the Algerian photographer Abdo Shanan.**

RS: Abdo was very generous and trusting from the start, which is key to any collaboration. He gave me full access not only to his body of work but to his ideas, to his history. It's about struggling to belong to a place that you feel doesn't want you. I can relate to that in a way, given Algeria's history of colonization. During the making of the book, I looked at the history behind these uprooted feelings to better understand the experience of postcolonial struggle. I read Frantz Fanon for the first time. I read *The Wretched of the Earth* (1961) and *Black Skin, White Masks* (1952), which informed my editorial and design decisions. Later, I read *Colonial Trauma* (2021) by Karima Lazali, which ended up being part of the book.

DA: **That's an insert in the book?**

RS: Yes. It's a beautifully written insight into the psychopolitical effects of colonialism in Algeria. It fits very well in *Dry* because there are the personal stories and the collective reckoning with inherited trauma. Both Shanan, who is Algerian Black with mixed ethnic parentage, and the people he photographed are con-

fronting their conflict with belonging.
The book opens with a kind of descent.
We see his window. Then, we go down-
stairs into a cemetery, and it's silver ink
on black paper. Then, his hand and his
imaginative world. And then you start the
book.

DA: **You've named Samer Mohdad, the
Lebanese Belgian photojournalist,
visual artist, and writer, as an important influence.**

**RS**: Mohdad's *Mes Arabies* was essential
to my beginnings. It was a revelation see-
ing Arabs portrayed outside of an anthro-
pological and orientalist framework.
When I saw the work, I was just beginning photography. It was published in
1999. It's one of the oldest books in my
collection, actually. It's a very ambitious,
rare document of a specific time in the
Arab world. He journeyed around twelve
countries and documented humble people he met along the way. I find that
everyone in his book has pride and
respect. He doesn't fetishize or glorify his
subjects.

DA: **I'm curious about other books that
have inspired you.**

**RS**: I love Nadhim Ramzi's *Iraq: The Land
and the People* (1977). I relate to him a lot
because he was a graphic designer and
photographer, like me. He's one of the
rare photographers we know about from
the older generation, other than Latif Al
Ani from Iraq. Many photographers existed
and still exist, a huge variety, but it can be
a challenge to find and access their work.

And there's Maen Hammad's book
*Landing* (2023), which layers journal
entries, poetry, and images to talk about
Palestinian resistance through the eyes of
young skateboarders, framing the act of
skating as a purposeful escape. *Landing*
is one of the projects that continued to
evolve way after I began working on it.
Maen came to me with a group of images
to create a standard photobook, but after
I read some of his very eloquent writing,
I suggested he write more. A month or
two later, he came back to me with so
many insights about Palestine. He shared
facts; he shared stories, including his
personal stories; he shared poems he
wrote.

When you're dealing with a subject
such as Palestine, you want to inform
people about the geopolitical context of
the place and not just rely on their inter-
pretation of things. When I exhibited

Maen Hammad, *Untitled*,
2015. From *Landing*
(self-published, 2023)

I see this project as
helping to mitigate
the construction of
otherness.

this work in Italy, I emphasized to Maen
that some images need captions. For
example, a refugee camp that is the most
tear-gassed place in the world. The
museum fought to remove these captions.
They wanted to remove information
about who inflicted this pain—the
Israel Defense Forces—but they had no
problem with showing the Palestinian
victims.

DA: **What's next for Bound Narratives?**

**RS:** Bound Narratives is expanding. This
includes digitization, exhibitions of
photobooks and images in galleries and
pop-up spaces—like Takeover, in Beirut—along with talks and workshops
around the book form. I'm hoping to find
funds to create an online repository and
commission artists, writers, and academ-
ics to engage with the library. I prefer this
localization of situated knowledge. I
think universalism, more often than
evoking all of us, imposes one narrative
and determines its value. I see this project as helping to mitigate the construction of otherness—how we're always
creating barriers and categorizing others.

Dalia Al-Dujaili is a writer, editor, and producer based
in London.

# Illuminations

A long-awaited
anthology highlights
Black women in
British photography.

**Vanessa Peterson**

My first paid job in the cultural sector, in the mid-2010s, was in London at a national museum with an extensive collection of photography, along with printed ephemera, pamphlets, zines, and photobooks, made by British and international artists. I once stumbled across a box of leaflets promoting the work and activity of Black photographers supported by organizations such as London's Autograph ABP, established in 1988 to support and exhibit Black and Asian lens-based artists, and was struck that so many of the names in these materials were new to me. Who were these artists? What had become of them? And why was their work rarely mentioned in historical analyses?

***Shining Lights: Black Women Photographers in 1980s–90s Britain*** (**MACK, 2024; 448 pages, $65**), jointly edited by the photographer Joy Gregory and the art historian Taous Dahmani, seeks to answer such questions. The anthology is four decades in the making. In

1981, Gregory enrolled as a photography student at the Manchester School of Art, where she eventually met Araba Mercer, a fellow student. Their friendship deepened when the women became neighbors in London—where Gregory had recently become the first Black woman to study photography at the Royal College of Art—and they embarked on the publication of a book on Black women photographers in Britain. The women distributed callouts and requests to strangers and peers by placing ads in relevant newsletters; in response, they received slides, negatives, and photographs. But the book did not come to fruition—fundraising proved too challenging. Even so, their efforts were crucial in establishing a support network for those seeking to remedy the absence of Black women—and Black female mentors—in Britain's art world and academy.

*Shining Lights* is divided into sections exploring self-portraiture, family relationships, and community activism. The book succeeds by enabling photographers such as Sutapa Biswas, Gilane Tawadros (now director of London's Whitechapel Gallery), and Gregory to speak to the ingenuity and DIY spirit of that era in their own words. Hampered by a lack of funding and intersectional exclusions from the art world, they were forced to find innovative ways to make and exhibit their work. Resources and skills were shared in community darkrooms. Despite infamously being hung in a corridor of London's Institute of Contemporary Arts rather than in a main gallery space, the 1985 group show *The Thin Black Line*, curated by Lubaina Himid, came to be regarded as a landmark exhibition of art by Black and Asian women. Publishing was another way to establish lines of communication outside the white cube or museum model. Magazines—*Polareyes*, dedicated to Black women photographers, and *Black Phoenix*, edited by the artist Rasheed Araeen—sought to preserve artistic practices for posterity, as photographers experimented with materiality, used the camera as a form of self-documentation, and reckoned with photography's role in colonialism.

A chapter called "Together: Community and Activism" reveals the cyclical nature of political debate in the United Kingdom. Glynis Neslen's black-and-white pictures document protest in the London borough of Lambeth in 1987 as well as casual moments with her fellow artists Veronica Ryan, Merle Van den Bosch, and Armet Francis. Carole Wright also takes a documentary approach, in work that focuses on social life in Brixton, an area that is home to a large Black community and has recently changed due to gentrification and rapidly increasing home prices. Set in barbershops, community centers, and living spaces, her photographs often capture scenes of tenderness: a girl helping put on her younger sister's shoes, boys showing off their new fades. Eileen Perrier's color portraits and interiors from a trip to Ghana, replete with cool pinks and greens, accord subjects—a young woman in a lilac dress with arms folded, an older matriarch sitting outside her home—firm control over their likenesses. Her pictures remind me of my own time in Accra, with relatives, in rooms filled with board games and faded

This page:
Claudette Holmes,
*Shirley*, 1990; opposite:
Joy Gregory,
*Autoportrait*, 1990/2006
Courtesy the artists and
MACK

These photographers were working at a time when the theoretical frameworks around Blackness were radically expanding.

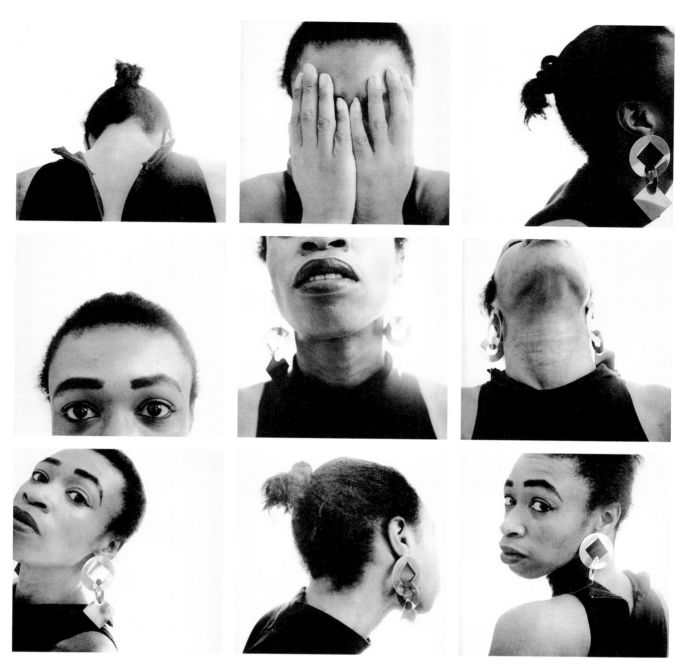

photographs, the sound of the women talking passing through our family home.

The photographers included in *Shining Lights* were working at a time when the theoretical frameworks and vocabulary around Blackness were radically expanding. Many of these artists seem to draw from the ideas of Paul Gilroy and Stuart Hall, whose writings on the Black Atlantic and "new ethnicities," respectively, broke ground in their critiques of essentialized definitions of race. African American cultural critics such as bell hooks were also influential. Of course, the meaning of *Black* continues to shift. As Gilroy writes,

"The idea that black is . . . an identity and collectively assembled in adverse circumstances and conditioned by the effects of systematic racism may no longer correspond to the brittle edifice of contemporary black struggle." This may be where younger readers will note the shifts in language and meaning over time. A roundtable included in the book features a later generation of photographers who acknowledge how anti-Blackness exists in different communities and that the meaning of the word *Black*—a political identity embraced in the 1980s and 1990s by "most 'othered' diasporas and people of colour,"

as Dahmani notes—has changed significantly in Britain in the past four decades.

"As Black women we have constantly endured other people telling our stories or explaining to us what we mean," Gregory writes in her introduction. *Shining Lights*, a vividly polyphonic and meticulously researched book, is a powerful corrective to such erasure—one that should be understood not as definitive but as ongoing, an invitation to reckon with how these stories are still being told today.

Vanessa Peterson is a writer and associate editor at *Frieze*.

# Reviews

## Mary Frey

Mary Frey's photographs from the late 1970s and early 1980s offer a lesson in the creative power of staying close to home. The microdramas that form her latest book, ***My Mother, My Son* (TBW, 2024; 72 pages, $50)**, an edit, from her archive, of images made over four decades, unfold in subtly menacing domestic interiors: aggressively patterned wallpapers induce vertigo; a baby sits unattended and vulnerable on a stark, improbably long sofa; two young men with Pre-Raphaelite flowing hair pose in a dungeon-like basement.

Snakes, birds, rabbits, and a ventriloquist doll are all found in or around the homes. Couples dance in front of a banal office building; groups of people gaze off into the distance, witnesses to events outside the frame. Her cast of white, middle-class suburbanites in Massachusetts consists of regular people doing slightly offbeat, irregular things. Though the pictures don't reach Diane Arbus heights of gnawing spectacle, disquiet lurks beneath the surface.

*Reading Raymond Carver*, the title of Frey's 2017 publication, invoked the influential short-story writer known for compressed, boozy vignettes filled with ordinary characters and quiet revelations. The

Cover of Mary Frey, *My Mother, My Son*. (TBW, 2024)

photograph's ability to hold a fiction exerts a strong pull on Frey, visible in the categories on her website: "Real Life Dramas," "Domestic Rituals." Fascinated by the tension between things as they are and things as they can be before the lens, she works with a large-format camera but wields it with on-the-fly immediacy.

*My Mother, My Son* is a modest book, some thirty images, flexibound, with the feel of a vintage family album. Its title derives from a 2004 photograph, included at the end—a startling coda—of Frey's son carrying his extremely frail grandmother. Frey tends to use a light touch when posing and sequencing her subjects, but this image, shorn of any affectation, is a gut punch of realism. —**Michael Famighetti**

---

## Sebastian Riemer

Sebastian Riemer's ***Press Paintings* (Spector, 2023; 312 pages, $40)** is, to a great degree, just what its contents appear to be: black-and-white news photographs that were retouched during their commercial production process to emphasize some elements of an image and eliminate others. In Riemer's hands, they have been further manipulated by digital means and blown up to sometimes massive scale. The strategy is right out of the Pictures Generation, except in this case the appropriated material is already so roughly reworked, to such slapdash and artless effect, that it was transformed long before Riemer, a German artist, got hold of it. Collected in a book, their original scale more or less restored, the pictures are fascinatingly weird, at once ordinary and twisted: raw Dada. Although Riemer's source material was made at the height of the picture press (1920s to 1960s), the imagery is stripped of any identification, and this anonymity allows it to slip its moorings—to enter a dream world. The retouching process encourages this sense of woozy unreality, ridding pictures of anything not strictly to the purpose of the articles they were meant to illustrate. Typically, that means isolating the subject of the photograph—a boxer, a socialite, a showgirl, an Etruscan vase—and overpainting or x-ing out everything else. The results suggest Andy Warhol, Richard Prince, or David Salle readymades, but cruder and, paradoxically, often quite elegant.

Most of Riemer's choices here are editorial; he's got an eye for the arresting, unsettling image. Occasionally, he stutters

Cover of Sebastian Riemer, *Press Paintings* (Spector, 2023)

or ghosts a picture, but usually he simply enlarges and re-presents photographs he found on the internet, minus identifying names, dates, locations, circumstances. With few narrative clues and no context except what we can imagine, the pictures are tantalizingly empty vessels, full of gorgeous abstract passages. In a conversation published in the book, David Campany reminds Riemer of Jeff Wall's take—"a feminist riposte"—on Sherrie Levine's rephotographed Walker Evans series, summing up that "whatever photography appropriates, it also points to." Riemer agrees but suggests there's a more layered and intuitive "performance" involved. For the cadence, the end, he says, "the enduring renewal of all imagery keeps them floating." —**Vince Aletti**

## Rahim Fortune

Hardtack is a saltless, cracker-like biscuit with a seemingly eternal shelf life, once rationed to the likes of sailors and soldiers in the US Civil War ("It tastes like sawdust," says a character in Percival Everett's novel *James*, set in the antebellum South). It's been nicknamed "survival bread." As the title of Rahim Fortune's new monograph, ***Hardtack* (Loose Joints, 2024; 144 pages, $63)**, it's a metaphor for sustenance, an ancestral food, a cultural madeleine.

Fortune is from the Chickasaw Nation of Oklahoma and was also raised in Texas. His two previous photobooks, *Oklahoma* (2020) and *I can't stand to see you cry* (2021), revisit the places and people of his upbringing with clarifying grace and a wisdom that is refreshingly without sentiment. With *Hardtack*, he enlarges that vision to include the American South as a whole. An unhurried casualness inhabits Fortune's subtle and stunning black-and-white photographs, inviting slowed-down looking. To quote the North Carolina poet Tyree Daye, from a poem that also dwells

in rural Black community: "We have removed the clocks so there is time."

Time to trace the captionless emblems—a sanitized pulpit, a gleaming vintage car, a holdout barbecue joint in a gentrifying city, a hat over the heart. Time to be enveloped in ritual—of praise dancing and quilting; of adornment of hair and dress and tattoo; of play and rest; of wind whipping through tall grass, a whisper across eras. Time to pull over at an innocuous hardware store—in a Texas town named for the major general who enforced the Emancipation Proclamation on June 19, 1865, and trace a current to the twenty-first-century Juneteenth riders who take five inside a rodeo ring, their boots tipped up along a cattle gate in brotherly sync.

*Hardtack* follows spiritually in the footsteps of Les Blank, whose films documenting idiosyncratic music and subcultures in the 1970s were a formative influence on Fortune, spurring him to photograph the rites and roots of Southern, Black, and Indigenous communities in the United States, to preserve the past for the future. Fortune charts a long arc for himself and this ongoing work. "Capturing and then sharing special moments," he

This page and page 129:
Spreads from Stephanie
Syjuco, *The Unruly Archive*
(Radius Books, 2024)

once wrote, "leaves proof that we were here." —**Rebecca Bengal**

---

## Stephanie Syjuco

Within Western institutions, archival and photographic material pose certain challenges, particularly given the way the camera has been wielded historically as a weapon of imperialism. Ariella Aïsha Azoulay notes that "turning to an item in the archive doesn't immediately rationalize what is seen." This is very much the problem the Philippine-born artist Stephanie Syjuco encountered when she began digging into the Smithsonian National Museum of American History's archives to research visual evidence of Filipinos and Filipinx Americans, only to realize the depth of their erasure.

***Stephanie Syjuco: The Unruly Archive*** (**Radius Books, 2024; 312 pages, $65**), Syjuco's first monograph, re-creates the experience of sifting through a physical record of documents, photographs, and other ephemera, while exploiting its unreliability. Designed to look like an archival box used in museum storage, the hardcover book contains not only the art-

ist's discoveries but also interventions to disrupt and recontextualize archives pertaining to the Philippines—a US colony for almost half a century—and its diaspora. The pages, cut to replicate assorted image sizes and sandwiched within semblances of manila folders, underscore the fragmentation and compartmentalization of a broader yet incomplete history.

Syjuco's intentional acts—collaging, cropping, enlarging, layering—allow the archives to, in her words, "talk back." Using Photoshop's "healing brush" tool to create a series titled *Blind Spot* (2023), she airbrushes Filipinos out of nineteenth- and early twentieth-century ethnographic photographs they may never have consented to be in, leaving behind only distortions and shadows. In other instances, her hands enter the frame to shield their faces, thus thwarting their dehumanization by a white colonial gaze. Although the project centers around the heritage to which she bears a direct connection, she invites nine other artists—including Carmen Winant, Savannah Wood, Wendy Red Star, and Pio Abad—to contribute essays and images, suggesting that hers is but one of many reclaimed narratives among colonized people. Syjuco's unique

art object not only invites viewers to flip through again and again but also leaves us wondering what infinite number of stories still lie dormant in dusty boxes, waiting for their turn to speak. —**Mimi Wong**

## Yorgos Lanthimos

In *Poor Things*, Yorgos Lanthimos's 2023 film, the mad scientist Godwin Baxter resurrects a drowned corpse to create Bella Baxter, a beautiful woman whose brain he has replaced with that of an infant. Played by Emma Stone, Lanthimos's frequent collaborator, Bella is an experiment in self-actualization. What does the self—curious, questing—look like when allowed to pour forth without having experienced neither cynicism nor lack?

"Although created on the set of the film *Poor Things* in Budapest, the book inhabits a separate world, untethered from time and place," notes the press release for Lanthimos's ***Dear God, the Parthenon is still broken*** (Void, 2024; 120 pages, $73.50). Yet no real effort has been made to distinguish the two: the photobook takes its title from a postcard Bella sends to Godwin in a scene cut from the fin-

ished film. Actors appear in costume; portraits and scenes are recognizably staged. This world is not separate from *Poor Things* but a continuation of it. By exposing the making of the film, Lanthimos dramatizes the system of art making at scale—what is artistic collaboration but an example of the self's emergent properties?

Shot with a large-format camera and developed in a makeshift bathroom darkroom by Lanthimos and Stone, the painterly, Deborah Turbeville–esque photographs of *Dear God* captivate in their stillness. The book makes clever but sparing use of double gatefolds, which expose the artificiality of the massive sets. A desert pit in Alexandria is, in fact, indoors, under a canopy of lights; a silken sunset is revealed to be a giant cyclorama. Lanthimos's portraits of his star surface a slippery tension between actress and character: in some, she is Stone, and in some, she is Bella. It's hard to determine how one knows; one just does. In pulling back the curtain, Lanthimos doesn't uncover the real behind the unreal but, as so many photographers have done before him, uses the camera to destabilize that binary, suggesting that life and fiction are not so separate either. —**Larissa Pham**

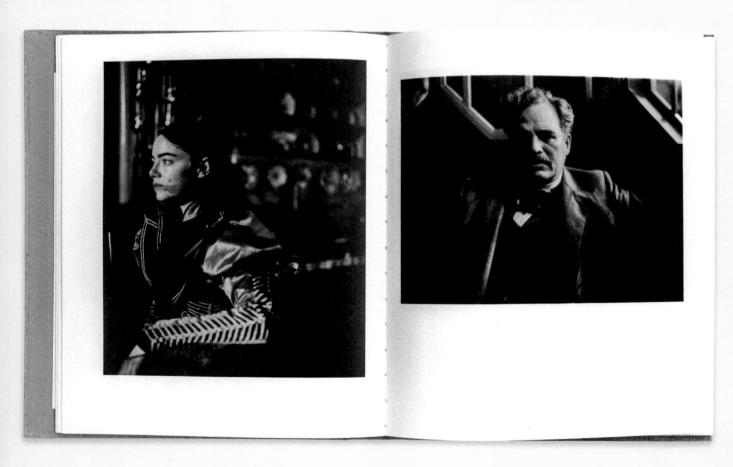

## Las Mexicanas

Stroll through any of Mexico's flea markets and you're sure to find boxes of vintage photographs amid antique silverware, tin plates, watches, buttons, and other ephemera. It's difficult to resist the urge to pore over these visual relics and wonder about the people in the pictures, or the photographs' prior owners. Stripped of any context, all is pure voyeuristic conjecture.

In **Las Mexicanas (Editorial RM, 2023; 136 pages, $25)**, the photographer Pablo Ortiz Monasterio edits such found images into a vivid narrative of female empowerment that's also a testament to the evolution of photography in Mexico from the mid-nineteenth century to the 1960s. These pictures, together with a searching essay by the sociologist Brenda Navarro, invite the reader to imagine the stories of the women being depicted: Are they members of the ruling class? Or descendants of Indigenous and African women murdered over the course of Mexico's violent history? Or ancestors of today's victims of femicide?

*Las Mexicanas* is a feat of curation—a photobook uniting otherwise disparate intimate family portraits and candid photographs to create a visual dialogue across social strata and historical time, asserting these women's hard-won protagonism throughout their country's history. "What is Mexico without the women who have been born in this land?" asks Navarro. "Beyond Mexico are the women; before the darkness of the birth of a nation, there is life that illuminates and makes way. And that obsession with persisting, because these women persist, not only emanates from those who photographed them but also from a kind of destiny: an ephemerality that yearns to be eternal."

Pocket-size, and with imagery ranging from formal studio portraits to spontaneous street snapshots to erotica, *Las Mexicanas* invites readers to meet the gazes of women who are by turns austere, expectant, coquettish. Fashions change over the decades, but what unites the women in *Las Mexicanas* across time and space, Navarro argues, is an acute sense that every passing joy captured on film is the counterpoint to some deep wound. Even so, viewed as a collective, *las mexicanas* exude a tenacious, irrepressible vitality. —**Elianna Kan**

# Endnote
## Rachel Kushner

In her writing about life on the margins, Rachel Kushner has established herself as a storyteller of devastating precision and unsentimental compassion. Her new novel, *Creation Lake* (2024), finds the author revisiting themes of revolution, agency, and betrayal, linking a French anarchist collective with the mysterious caves of early humans.

***Creation Lake* weaves together an espionage thriller with an epistolary treatise on the shadowy origins of humanity. What led you to the origins narrative?**
The human world "before the written down" has always been a site of fantasy, psychoanalytic projection, and pure speculation: ideal subject matter for the novelist, or so you'd think, and yet few novelists have ventured into that territory. I got interested in prehistory and how developments in the genetic mapping of early humans were completely upending what everyone thought they knew. Suddenly, we had all this evidence of when Neanderthals and *Homo sapiens* interbred. With new technologies and discoveries, DNA is now an encoding of a person's entire vast ancestral and evolutionary history: each person a saga of eons, of extraordinary proportions.

**The book follows an American spy who infiltrates a French commune of radical eco-activists. Why are you drawn to outsiders?**
I had long wanted to set a novel in a rural commune of urban anarchists who decamp from Paris to organize their own collective society. Southwestern France is a region I know well; I spend every

summer there, and it's a terrain that happens to be subtended by an underground world of caves. I chose as my narrator a woman, alias Sadie, who works undercover for some consortium of people, whether government or private enterprise. She insinuates herself among the anarchist collective and thinks she's going to set them on a collision course with French police. At the same time, she becomes focused on the group's mentor, Bruno Lacombe, who lives in a cave and is the real and true outsider.

**Are you a longtime reader of noir?**
No, not so much. But a couple of years ago I fell in love with the crime novels of Jean-Patrick Manchette. Now I've read much more, including the Americans who influenced him.

**Blindness is a central motif of the book, and Bruno experiments with the pursuit of enlightenment via total darkness.**
Bruno Lacombe longs to escape capitalism, which he believes will never be dismantled or overthrown. The only solution is a kind of radical renovation of consciousness itself. But in his sojourn into darkness, his mind is flooded with images, as if he can never be free of the

world he comes from. Ironically, among what he sees very clearly is a photograph of Helen Keller, an image in his memory bank that returns to him in the dark. He sees what Helen Keller cannot. The details of this photograph came to me while writing because the artist and filmmaker James Benning had included the Keller photograph in *ALABAMA*, a show he made in 2022. She's seated so regally, with an enormous magnolia blossom in her lap: a blind woman apprehending all these qualities of the flower that are available to her and perhaps enhanced by her inability to see.

**Your epigraph comes from Shakespeare: "Close, in the name of jesting! Lie thou there, for here comes the trout that must be caught with tickling."**
It's a scene from *Twelfth Night*. Trout tickling there is a metaphor, but in my novel it's literal: Bruno learned to handfish as a boy, and recollects the patience and expertise of catching trout with his bare hands. I've heard people reject handfishing as a legend or myth. But it's real. I've seen it. My narrator takes from Bruno's account of trout tickling the idea that you don't actively seduce in order to manipulate people. You put your hand in the water, and you wait.